Acknowledgements

To everyone who struggles. Whether it be through fears and phobias or any kind of mental health.

Face your fear.
There is always help and support out there, you are not alone.

FEAR TRIGGER

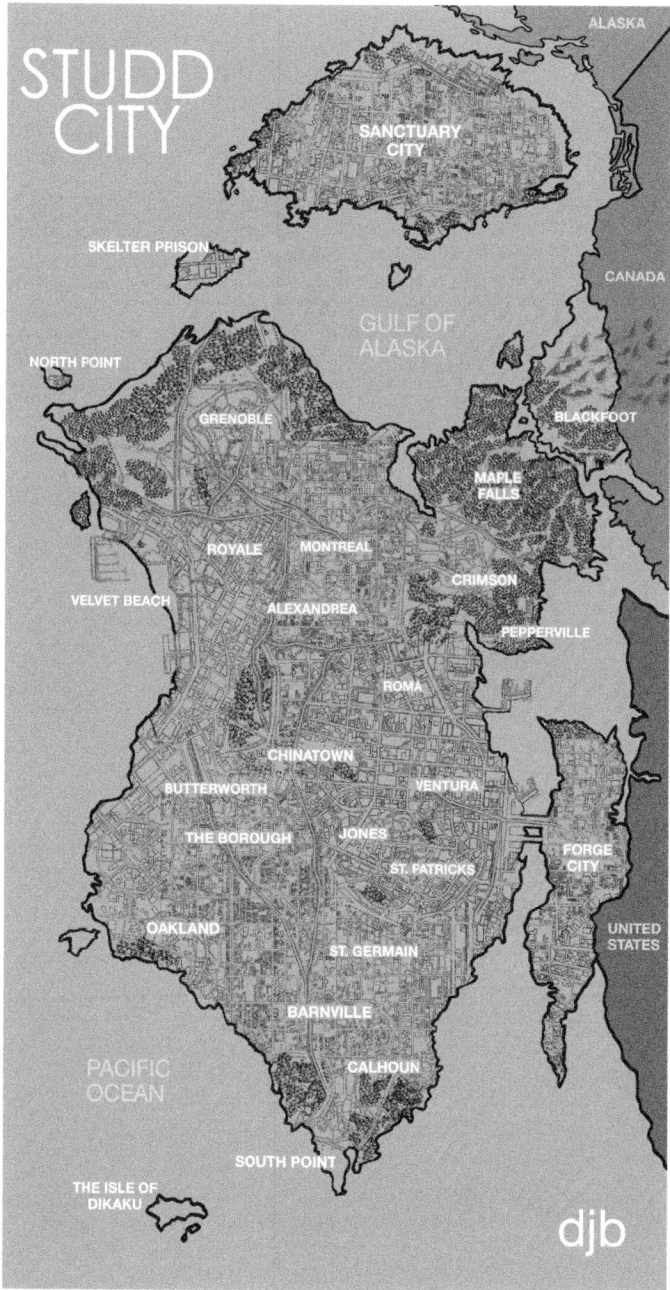

STUDD CITY

ALASKA

SANCTUARY CITY

SKELTER PRISON

CANADA

GULF OF ALASKA

NORTH POINT

GRENOBLE

BLACKFOOT

MAPLE FALLS

ROYALE   MONTREAL

CRIMSON

VELVET BEACH

ALEXANDREA

PEPPERVILLE

ROMA

CHINATOWN

BUTTERWORTH   VENTURA

THE BOROUGH   JONES

ST. PATRICKS

FORGE CITY

OAKLAND

UNITED STATES

ST. GERMAIN

BARNVILLE

PACIFIC OCEAN

CALHOUN

SOUTH POINT

THE ISLE OF DIKAKU

djb

CHAPTER 1

The solid oak door stood centre stage in the middle of the modern art gallery. Its vibrant red glaze shimmered under the bright spotlights that seemed to attack it from every angle. Every painstaking brush stroke seemed accounted for, and consumed every inch of what appeared to be a normal every day front door. Even the bronze door knob that was polished to its fullest was present, and the matching letter box which was cut into the oak halfway down the door. Above there was a door knocker present, protruding out of it proudly. The knocker was cast iron and as black as coal. Its shape was that of a black horse, a stallion, majestically rearing up on its hind legs. Each muscle intricately etched into the iron giving the illusion that the creature did indeed defy gravity, to show its dominance. The door itself was set in an oak frame, that had been heavily varnished, several layers in fact, making the wood appear much darker and under the constant glare of the spotlights, it appeared tacky, maybe even sticky to the touch, like the consistency of honey. But that was not all. This everyday normal looking door and frame was wrapped in a rust covered chain. Thick ageing links of chain coiled itself around the exhibit tightly, like some hungry boa constrictor, either looking to consume the door or protecting it from others getting their slippery scales on it. The chains were clamped tightly together by a hefty padlock, just your average everyday padlock that could be purchased at most good hardware stores. There was no key in the lock, its whereabouts remained a mystery, but cut into this particular lock were the letters J and H, initials, a signature in fact, the calling card of popular artist and sculptor Jack Heron. Jack Heron stood casually observing this monstrous piece of art,(or what was being perceived as art) his arms crossed around his tall slender frame. A mop of auburn hair falling across one side of his face and concealing the tired sunken sockets that were occupied by two jade pools. Stood adjacent to Jack was a woman Marcy Nolan. A strong looking woman, ballsy and stern but pretty, dressed in a trouser suit which fitted snuggly in all the right places to accentuate her slender figure and her long legs. She was Jack's agent and oldest friend. The two had met years ago at university in London when they were growing into adulthood. She admired Jack and his work and always steered him in the right direction. They were very good friends, very close, but not involved. Jack often thought that he would like to be involved with Marcy, he adored her American accent and how she pronounced his surname (*Hair-on*), always made him smile. However it was one of those feelings that he just bottled up and dismissed, she wouldn't be interested in him he had often thought. He had never really had any luck with women, well with a sex life in general. He had no sex life, he hadn't had sex, not really, it just had never happened. He had problems in that department and because of that had often thought that he was maybe homosexual. But, he had found that he wasn't attracted to men at all, maybe he was Asexual. He had read an article about Asexuality at some point and thought that he may well have been that, it was possible he supposed. Its meaning being a lack of interest in sex but that didn't feel right to him, he couldn't be could he? He had had sex hadn't he? He couldn't remember, he remembered the caressing touch of fingers on his erect penis, but nothing else. Did that happen or was it purely imagination? He couldn't say. No, he was probably not Asexual and he wasn't Homosexual. He knew that his assistant Robin was gay and had sometimes thought about asking whether you can tell if someone else is or not, but he thought he'd look stupid. But then there was Marcy, he loved Marcy. He would love to... be with her he thought, he often thought that.

"I don't know," Jack said, a long slender index finger digging at the sheep's wool turtleneck jumper, that itched his neck, "I'm still not sure."

"You'd better be fucking sure!" Marcy scoffed, "The exhibit opens in five days!"

"I know!" He snapped and then sighed.

"Ever the perfectionist!" Laughed Marcy, her short dark bob fluttered as she shook her head.

"You fucking artists are a pain in the keister!" She smiled and it was warming.

"Yeah, I guess we are." He said, smiling back. They continued staring at the door that seemed to rise out of the floor like some gigantic eyesore, well that's what Jack thought it looked like. Behind him a gangly looking man scuttled around, his hips shimmying in rapid succession as his legs seemed to move even faster than he did. His heeled leather shoes clipped across the white tiled floor as he went. He looked flustered carrying several framed oil canvases as he moved along. Jack turned as he heard the man approaching and gave him a smile, the flustered man smiled back.

"How's it going, Robin?" He asked, still scratching at his neck with his rugged fingernail, that had become bitten down after a stressful week of preparing the gallery.

"Okay, Mr Heron. Nearly there!" Robin answered in a pleasant and enthusiastic voice.

"Please call me Jack, Robin okay?"

"Sure!" He smiled and then hurried away to continue with his duties, which were plenty when you were the personal assistant for a well known artist, who in fact had a new gallery opening in New York City in less than a week. Jack had turned his attentions back to the door but was still talking to Robin.

"Much too formal to keep calling me Mr Heron all the time."

"You do know he's gone don't you?" Said Marcy.

"What?" Jack said turning to look at her, seemingly miles away, "Who?"

"Forget it!" She replied with a rolling of her eyes. She was used to him getting like this when he was either thinking about creating art, making art or observing art, which was pretty much all the time. She often wondered where he would go when he spaced out like this.

"Stop deconstructing it for heaven's sake will you!" She groans and gives him a nudge, which causes him to sway from side to side, like some long pendulum on a Grandfather clock, still seemingly oblivious to her.

"Sorry, what?"

"I give up!" She sighed, "You're impossible Jack Heron!"

Jack immediately smiled.

Hair on he thought.

"Don't take the piss!" She knew what that look meant. She laughed and nudged him again. This time he put a caring arm around her and gave her a squeeze.

"You think they'll like it?" He asked.

"Are you crazy?" She looked at him a little perplexed. She had worked with a number of creative types over the years, authors, actors, dancers, artists and it always confused her when these talented individuals would dislike their work and never think it was good enough. Fear she had often thought. The fear is what holds them back from potential, it's as though they can't see the woods for the trees.

"We've had a hell of a positive response from the 'so called' experts and connoisseurs of the art world. You're on fire at the moment Jack!"

"Well, that's good then." He says unenthusiastically, miles away again. His eyes surveying every brush stroke, every grain in the wood.

"Jesus! Calm down! You might give yourself a hernia getting all overexcited like that!" She laughed.

"What?" He grumbled again.

She rolled her eyes at him again. The trip trapping of Robin's shoes skipped across the floor as he hurried passed them again, flustered and busy, murmuring to himself all the things he had to get done. He passes the white walls that home the work of Jack Heron, mainly paintings, he had mostly been known for his acrylic pieces, mostly focussing on horses or water and in some cases the two were

11

combined. He was often asked in interviews or just intrigued fans of his work why he only ever seemed to paint water and horses. He never had an answer for them, he usually just shrugged, but that was the correct answer. It wasn't some sordid mystery or secret he was keeping to work the people, to make them think it was some gimmick, where he was a little zany and aloof. Sure he was a little aloof but he couldn't honestly say why he painted the things that he did. He was once challenged by some art magazine to paint a self portrait. As he had never painted a portrait in his life before he accepted the challenge, but the finished piece was rather strange to say the least. He had painted the closeup of a black horse's head, its eye fiery and full of colour. He was looked upon as crazy for a while until someone online had discovered that his portrait was there after all. It was amazingly contained in that fiery marble of the horse's eye, as if it was Jack's own reflection. This took the art world by storm and he was showered with praise and given the awkward title of 'genius'. That moniker seemed to hang like a weight around his neck as he went back to painting his water and his horses again, much to the displeasure of the art world that were only months ago singing his praises. The fickle world that lies in wait to diminish and demean peoples hard work. Jack didn't care, but Marcy did, being his agent and seeing he was capable of more and should give the people what they want. It was the only thing they had ever argued about, he wanted to do things for the love of doing it, where she saw it from the money making side. She finally talked him into trying something different, so he gave sculpturing a try. His first piece was phallic in its shape and Marcy did laugh when she first saw it. Jack did not see what was so funny about it, to him it was just something that he had shaped from clay and just happened to resemble a large erect male sex organ. She talked him into displaying it at his old gallery, which was in the middle of Forge City, a small little place which didn't really have the passing trade that he required. It went down a storm by lovers of erotic art and was actually purchased for $1.5 million by an eccentric and very wealthy man by the name of Robert Devine. Several other sculptures followed and always resembled the same sort of thing, an erect penis. Again he was the darling of the art world and was asked where the inspiration had come from for such pieces. Yet again he had no answer for them, because he didn't know. Next came his minimalist phase where he would create exhibits such as one entitled *'Love by Death and Death by Razor'* which had a bath plug hanging from a ridiculously long chain from the ceiling with a razor blade protruding from the end of it and red paint dripping from its tip onto the white tile below. It seemingly meant nothing to Jack, as did all his works. They meant nothing to him and he had no emotional attachment to any of it. But the door, now, the door was different. It seemed very different to him and he didn't know why. What did it mean? He tried to process this feeling, or whatever it was. This piece he had created meant something to him, maybe that's why he was being over critical about this certain piece? Marcy had left about five minutes ago to go for coffee. Somewhere a phone rang but it sounded distant. He took out his glasses that were concealed in the inside of his blazer pocket. They were designer in frame but the lenses were magnified, specifically used when he needed to get up close and personal to an art piece. He stared at the door through the lenses that caused the door to become distorted at certain angles. He lowered them and began to chew relentlessly on the temple tips of those very expensive pair of spectacles, his teeth chipping away on the plastic like a beaver would gnaw on the bark of a tree. He was almost hypnotised by the stallion shaped door knocker.

"Rat-a-tat-tat..." He whispered to himself and his brow contorted. He heard a voice from somewhere, *Robin* he thought, but didn't answer.

"Rat-a-tat-tat." He said again to himself.

He heard robin again, louder now, more urgent. Then there was Marcy's voice calling him, but still he did not acknowledge the voices. He could see them standing over by the reception desk through the reflection in the brass door knob and then the letterbox. He saw the hustle and bustle of New York going about its business through the gigantic glass front of the gallery. Marcy had taken the phone from Robin and was talking to whoever had called, she seemed to look sad and clawed at her forehead as if taking in important information.

"Rat-a-tat-tat?" He said again, almost asking himself what it meant and for a split second, he could have sworn that the chains that were wrapped tightly around the door twitched. Moved. Rattled.

"Rat-a..."

"Jack!" He heard Marcy, she was close now, not distant like before and he was snapped out of his musing.

"Yeah?" He asked solemnly, still not taking his eyes off the door.

"Did you not hear us calling you?"

"Yeah..." He said and then turned to see that something was worrying her.

"What's the matter?" He asked and looked over at Robin who was placing the phone back in its cradle and looking solemnly at Jack, "Is something wrong?"

"That was your family's solicitor, a Mr Butterworth?" She looked over at Robin for confirmation of the name, he shrugged at her.

"Butterworth? I don't know anyone called Butterworth?" He said.

"It's your family solicitor from back in the UK. Brace yourself Jack, but, your Grandfather has died."

"Rat-a-tat-tat!" Gasped Jack and then he fainted.

CHAPTER 2

Jack's head is hazy when he regains consciousness. Faces from a past he had all but forgotten dance in front of his minds eye, stuttering and obscure faces. Who were these people? At this moment in time he could not tell you, but he knew them. He heard Marcy's voice echo through his head, she sounded concerned, worried, but her voice was calming to him and slowly but surely he came around. Those faces that flickered before him faded into the faces of Marcy and Robin.

"Did you remember the sugar in my coffee this time?" He joked, rubbing at the back of his head as he sat up.

"Never mind that!" Marcy snapped.

"Are you okay?" She asked with some urgency.

"Yeah," He said, trying to get to his feet, "I think so."

"Let us help you." Said Robin, the words clumsily stuttering out from his throat, he was never good in situations like this. They helped him up and over to a chair near the reception desk. Jack swept his hair away from his face with a shaking hand.

"Okay?" Marcy asked again.

"Yeah, yeah!" He nodded, still looking a little out of it, but isn't that how he always looked?

"Robin, can you go and get him some water please?" She asked.

"Of course." He stuttered and tottered off to a hidden staff area at the other side of the gallery.

"What happen there, Jack?" She asked kneeling down in front of him. Her eyes contained so much love and care, he thought of diving into those two blue pools and then a thought popped into his head, b*ut you can't swim.*

He then looked at her oddly, through her.

Where did that come from?

"Are you still with me, Jack?" She asked again placing a hand on his knee.

"Yeah, I'm okay. Just fainted." He shrugged nonchalantly.

"I guess it was the shock." She nodded, her face looked full of pity for him.

"I guess." He shrugged again, a strange look of confusion consuming his face.

"Were you close to him?"

"What? Who?"

"Who? Why your Grandfather of course!"

"Oh, well, I guess I was once." He felt the rush of guilt flow over him in a hot sticky wave. He hadn't seen his Grandfather for around twenty years, in fact he probably hadn't even thought of any of his family since the day he left the family home.

Escaped is more like it! He thought to himself and then pondered this.

Why escaped?

In truth he couldn't really remember anything from his childhood, the first clear memories he had of life were at 16 when he left to join art college.

17

"To be completely honest with you Marcy, it's been so long that I can't really remember him." He felt so much guilt.

"Oh!" She said sadly.

"Does that make me sound like a complete bastard? It does, doesn't it?" He hung his head.

"No," She said smiling, and rubbing his knee.

"It's just been so long since that part of your life, you've been so busy and working so hard, it's just been pushed to one side unfortunately."

"I still feel like a bastard though. I could have... should have made the effort, but I just..." His thoughts pattered off somewhere, "Rat-a-tat-tat." He said absently as Robin arrived with a plastic cup filled with ice cold water from the dispenser in the staff area.

"Thanks Robin." He said taking the water and sipping it. Robin smiled, but still his furrowing brow displayed his concern.

"Feeling better?" Robin asked.

Jack nodded and smiled, it made Robin feel a little easier and his busy brow became visually less muddled.

"What did you say just now?" Marcy asked standing back up.

"I don't know," Jack shrugged again, "What did I say?"

"Ratta... tatta, something!" She shrugged.

"I really don't know. Was just like a knocking in my head. Rat-a-tat-tat."

Marcy and Robin looked at each other a little concerned.

"Did you bang your head when you fell, Jack?" She asked.

"No," He said shaking his head, "at least I don't think so."

"Maybe you did and you have a little concussion?" Said Robin.

18

"Don't be silly!" Jack laughed, "and please, both of you stop fussing over me! I'm fine, really I am!"

"Okay, okay!" Marcy replied holding her hands up in the air, indicating that there would be no more fussing.

"It's not like I don't appreciate the concern." He said and smiled at them both, "I just had some bad news that's all and fainted. I'm sure that's pretty common, isn't it?"

They both nodded in unison.

"Good, then let's move on shall we?"

They both smiled and Marcy rolled her eyes. Robin tottered off to carry on with what he was doing before all this had occurred. Jack continued to sip his water. It was extremely cold as it made its way down his throat, it felt like it was freezing everything it touched, but the chill was soothing and fought back any nausea he might have been feeling. He couldn't afford to be sick, Marcy would have him in the hospital before he could say Rat-a-tat-tat.

Rat-a-tat-tat? What the hell is that?

"I'll make the necessary arrangements for your flight to... England?" Marcy asked.

"Wales actually, a small town in the south of Wales called, Cyfrinach pwynt y De."

"Say what now?" She said looking confused.

"Is that even English?"

"No, it's Welsh." He said absently, "Wait a minute! What do you mean flight?"

"Your Grandfather just died, Jack! You've got to go and pay your respects and see your family."

19

"I have no other family. He was the last." Something flashed in his head again, a jumble of memories perhaps all fused together, attacked his brain all at once, like he was running through a tunnel. He felt sick but fought the urge again and sipped the water.

"Well, all the more reason to go and say goodbye to the old guy."

"But, the gallery is opening in…"

"It will keep!" She snapped interrupting him, "Somethings are more important."

"If you think it's for the best?"

"I do. Besides you've got to go anyway."

"Why is that?"

"You have to go for the reading of the will and sign some paperwork about your Grandfather's estate. Well, I guess it will be your estate now." He sighed, like it was all a hassle.

"I'm not going to want to keep that old bloody house anyway! Can't they just email me the paperwork to sign?"

"Apparently not! Mr Butterworth was very adamant that you went actually."

"Yeah, probably get's a big cut of the fortune."

"Probably, if he's been the family solicitor for all these years."

"Money grabbing bastard!"

"You'd do the same." She smirked.

"Yeah, you're probably right!" Jack laughed.

"He's only after his slice of the pie I guess."

"Good! I'll book you a flight then. You can be there and back in a couple of days and still be ready for the gallery's grand opening!"

"I guess." He felt sick again as a vision of the house came into his head. The house was dark and eery and seemed to call to him through the garnet coloured maw that was its entrance. It wasn't nausea or apprehension that he felt about this whole situation. Not sadness or irritation but fear. Fear to return to the house of his childhood, for revealing lost memories, for seeing the house again. Fear of remembering.

But why? Fear of what?

CHAPTER 3

The flights were hell, eight hours from New York to Amsterdam had been spent mostly in the compact casket known as the bathroom. His head was woozy and kept having mental flashes that he could only presume were old memories, events that he had obviously forced to the back of his mind to forget about. Jack couldn't work them out or understand what it was all about. None of the visions were clear yet, but what had become clear was the constant flowing of vomit that kept spewing out of his mouth. The fasten your seat belt sign that flickered on and off several times through the flight, meant nothing to Jack as he spent the time clinging on to the bowl of the lavatory. He was pretty much left to his own devices, occasionally a stewardess would tap the door and ask him if he was okay, but after answering only in grunts, groans and dry heaves, they finally gave up. He imagined the heavily made up faces gurning from the vile sounds gurgling from his raw throat, he chuckled a little to himself, finding humour in the image of their make up cracking as they sneered in disgust. The only sleep he had managed came at the Amsterdam airport as he waited for his next flight to Cardiff. His stomach was empty and he basically collapsed in a chair at the gate. Luckily for him there was time to kill before his next flight. He dreamt while he was there, but again nothing was clear, nothing concrete to go on. There was the soft rippling of water, it looked almost green to him with the consistency of thick soup. Something floated underneath the water, like the slow flickers of an octopus's tentacles, reaching toward him from deep down below. It looked organic though and almost plantlike, seaweed perhaps, Algae? Stoneworts? Whatever it was it seemed to reach for him. Suddenly two eyes appeared looking back at him and that was enough to wake him from his slumber.

The Dutch voice had echoed through the tannoy and woken him. He was very glad of this as he sat there sweating profusely, before repositioning himself on the chair, being mindful to clutch his only piece of luggage, which happened to be a worn brown leather carry on that he had had since his university days.

He had fallen back to sleep, that is when he had seen the horse, the black horse. It was stood pretentiously on a field, silhouetted against a congested sky. The shape of the stallion looked menacing as it stared at Jack. A thick layer of mist had risen up from the dewy grass, covering its hooves, pasterns and cannons, almost rising to the knee. It seemed to give the illusion that it was hovering above the moist grass, a majestic steed floating on a blanket of vapour. It snorted and its warm breath attacked the cold air and rose up evaporating quickly. Jack remembered shuddering in his sleep. The sun was coming up behind the stallion, but the sky seemed almost green/blue in the light and that's when he caught sight of the horse's eye. Black and angry, gleaming with flecks of green like some gigantic marble reflecting that strange eery sky. The horse stomped its large heavy hoof onto the moist ground and he felt the ground shake beneath him, and then a violent rumbling sound filled his

23

head. He caught his reflection in the eye, the portrait he had painted was now in his minds eye but perversely his face started to change and manifest into other faces. His Grandfather.

Finally he could see his face clearly again, the name to the face came and the name William touched his lips. Before he could remember anymore, the face started to change again. A lady screamed at him, then it immediately changed to an old wart covered man in a flat cap sneering at him. Then quickly it changed again and now a young boy opened his mouth and a green tinted liquid, thick like treacle oozed from his gaping maw. He shuddered again and felt tears running down his face. But still the faces changed. A beautiful black female in a maid's mob cap smiled seductively at him, he felt sick again. The face changed again to another woman, tears streaming down her gaunt features, the tears becoming blood and dripping down in freshets. The paint from the portrait now dripping, as if it were melting. It changed once more before it became just a mush of colour. The face of a man that looked skeletal and diseased, as if something had eaten away at his face.

"Father!" He had remembered screaming and then waking up to see a bunch of people gathered around him, seeing if he was okay and informing him it was time to board the plane.

The train journey from Cardiff to Cyfrinach pwynt y De passed without a hitch. He didn't vomit or feel in the least bit sick anymore and he didn't sleep, he daren't. The train was vintage you might say, like the old trains you would see in some *Agatha Christie* movie. He smiled to himself, he liked that. No modern trains ran out this far south, not to the small town of Cyfrinach pwynt y De anyway. Not many people came out this way in fact, there was only this one particular train that ran the route each day. There was just not the demand to come where there was seemingly nothing for anyone. Jack thought about the dreams he had had and tried to work out what they meant. They felt familiar to him but again, he couldn't quite put his finger on what they meant. He had theorised that the melting faces could have been the gathering crowd of people that had circled him. It was possible that he had been half asleep and seen them gawping at him through squinted eyes. He looked out at the beautiful countryside that Wales had to offer and he felt at peace. The steam train trundled along at a nice pace so he could take in the exquisite surroundings that are known affectionately as, The Valleys. He was glad that it wasn't one of these modern contraptions that were built for speed and were so fast you missed the real beauty of this world as it flashed past in blurs of blue and green. It finally struck him that the vomiting was not caused by travel sickness as he had initially thought, or maybe even food poisoning but through anxiety. Something inside him had become so worked up that it had initially caused him to vomit. He remembered that he had first felt the goring sensation at the gallery when he had learnt about his Grandfather's death. It wasn't the grief that made him feel that way, in his own way he had already grieved for his Grandfather because it had been twenty years since he had last seen or heard from him. It was if he had already died. It was if he had already grieved for all his family that had passed on, so no it wasn't grief that caused all of this. He felt right as rain now as he sat on the train, like nothing had ever happened to him. There was still a feeling that lingered though, like a bad smell in the air, like he had trodden in dog mess and was unable to scrape it all off and some of it had stayed with him burning his nostrils every now and again.

"It's fear!" He suddenly said to himself, luckily nobody else was sitting in his carriage to hear him talking to himself like a madman. The anxiety that had built up inside him and made him ill was out of fear. All the visions and dreams, were born out of fear.

Fear of what? Returning home? Family? But my family are all dead.

That thought hung around for a while. The apparitions that he had seen in his dream, they were his family, visions of his home and his past.

But what happened to them? Why can't I remember?

He rested his head against the carriage's window, the feel of the glass was cold on his temple, but invigorating to his head that throbbed with constant distress. The cogs ground together working double time to find answers, answers that were needed to make some sense of all that was going on. As the carriage gently rocked from side to side in a comfortable motion, Jack started to drift again.

CHAPTER 4

Rat-a-tat-tat!

Was the sound he suddenly heard, that sequence tapped out in that same haunting rhythm that obviously meant something to him, but what did it mean?

Rat-a-tat-tat!

It came again, louder than before, or was it closer? Had it chimed through his head from a distance? There was a loud roaring from the trains whistle and Jack's eyes exploded out from the safe confines of their lids and was met again by the sound, Rat-a-tat-tat! A small rotund man was tapping on his window with the business end of a very expensive looking walking stick. He was face to face with a silver horse's head handle looking back at him as it scraped at the glass.

"Mr Heron?" Came the muffled voice from the other side of the window. Jack tried to gather himself and his bearings, he had no way of knowing how long he had been asleep for, it could have only been minutes for all he had known. He looked around outside and it was indeed the station for Cyfrinach pwynt y De. There was no need to hurry to go anywhere as this was the end of the line for this particular locomotive.

"I say, sir," The muffled voice came again, "are you Mister Jack Heron?"

"Yes!" Jack shouted, a little too loud that he made himself jump.

"Ah! Good show!" The man smiled, a crooked smile packed into an ageing chubby face.

"Mr Butterworth!" He announced.

Jack nodded and grabbed his bag and exited the train. He stepped off the train and was suddenly ambushed by an array of smells, old but familiar smells. Memories immediately came flooding back, as if someone had yanked his head sideways and had begun pouring them into his brain using a funnel and jug. The memories of course were too much to take in at one time, his weary mind not having the capacity to deal with so much information at once, that most of the images where spat right back out. What he did remember though was the smell of the coal and the soot, he'd smelt that before when he left at the ripe old age of 16. That was it, he had come of age and was headed to the best art college that the family fortune could buy. He remembered that he had little to stay for, there was nothing to offer here. His Grandfather the only living relative to stay for... *Grandad William!* He thought, It was if he couldn't remember his name. Jack Heron had fought so hard to forget about this place that he had inadvertently forgotten his own Grandfather's name. Guilt came, then fear, then the threat of vomit again. He felt physically sick and ashamed. He had come of age and ran away to the city, to the big time and forgot about what he had left behind. Or was this the truth? Was that a hundred percent the truth? Or did he run away? He had to leave, wanted to leave. But did he run? Did he escape? There was hardly anyone on the platform and the whole place seemed to be encased in a dome of subtle mist. It felt like a gigantic snow globe and he was trapped inside. That fabulous Welsh breeze drifted in through the valleys and doused his face, again memories came with it, too many to focus on, too many to remember.

"Good day, Mr Heron!" Mr Butterworth beamed as he waved a leather gloved hand at Jack as he stepped down onto the platform. Butterworth didn't attempt to move forward to greet him, he just waited for Jack to approach. He was extremely smartly dressed in a three piece tweed suit with a fedora balanced neatly on top of his head. His walking cane had wedged itself into a crack in the platform, absorbing all the weight of his hefty bulk as he casually leant on it.

"Pleased to meet you, Mr Butterworth." Jack said smiling with a hand out stretched.

"Charmed!" Butterworth said taking his hand and shaking it firmly.

"Well, this place hasn't changed!" Jack scoffed.

"Indeed. It has been some time since you have been home I understand?" Butterworth asked, his face beaming with that smile again. His face was so round and red that it looked like a balloon that had swollen up with air so much that it was about to pop.

"Yeah, it's been around twenty years."

"It's really been as long as that?" Butterworth made a tutting sound and shook his head in disbelief. The small talk had come abruptly to an end with neither man having anywhere to go after that.

"So, what's the plan?" Jack said with a shrug, throwing his bag over his shoulder, giving a huge hint that he would indeed like to move the process on.

"Of course." Butterworth nodded and began to walk towards the exit of the station. He heard the train backing out of the station slowly, clouds of black smoke exploded from its stumpy chimney and the station master (that also happened to be the porter, the signalman and any other job going) waddled back to his office, snatching at a bottle of Scotch that he'd left on an empty bench. Jack watched as the ticket office door closed behind him and through the window he saw the soles of two worn boots as they landed unceremoniously on a desk and crossed over each other. His day of work was done. Butterworth strode ahead, flicking out his cane in front of him arrogantly with each step. Jack had to quicken his pace to keep up with the aggressive stride of the little plump man as he traipsed onto the cobbled road that lead into the town of Cyfrinach pwynt y De. It looked deserted apart from a few pottering around, they stared at Jack with inquisitive eyes.

"As you may or may not know I have been The Heron family solicitor for quite sometime now. My Father was very good friends with your Grandfather and when my Father passed on, about ten years ago now..."

"My condolences!" Jack interrupted.

"Thank you." Butterworth nodded acknowledging the gesture.

"Well, he always told me that I should look after The Heron Family. Treat them with the upmost respect and loyalty, whatever happens."

"What did he mean by 'whatever happens'?" Asked Jack.

"Oh nothing my boy! Nothing at all!" Butterworth chuckled.

Jack knew he was lying or at least hiding something.

"So that is what I have always done." Butterworth beamed proudly.

It was a very picturesque town, but it looked as though time had passed it by. It may be that the modern world of cell phones, computers and the internet have just not reached this part of the world yet, or because Jack had spent the last twenty years of his life in gigantic cities, that moved a hundred miles a minute, that he was just not accustomed to the slower pace of the countryside. The houses looked quaint but crooked, as though they were all leaning on each other for support. The interiors of most of the homes were hidden by squares of cheap voile and Jack could see them twitch as he passed each house. He felt dirty and used, all those cynical eyes leering at him, thinking things about him. The wagging of deceptive tongues already casting assumptions. There was that nauseating feeling again in his throat, and vomit seemed to bubble up and attempt to explode, but Jack swallowed hard and forced it back down from where it came.

Jack you're being paranoid! They're just being nosey, you're a new face in their town, have they every right to be a bit inquisitive. Still that paranoia though, why does it scare me so? Why the fear?

"Where are we going?" Jack asked.

"Just to my office," Said Butterworth "it's only a short walk up the high street." And he waved his walking cane in the air to the direction of the office.

"How long is all this going to take? I do need to get back to the states quite sharpish. I have a new gallery opening in a few days you see and..."

31

"Oh, it shouldn't take long, my boy." Butterworth intervened, he had obviously heard enough and did not seem the slightest bit interested in Jack's life.

"There is an awful lot to discuss though, the reading of the will and what you would like to do with estate and..."

"I don't care!" Jack snapped, it was his time to interrupt, and this startled Butterworth so much so, that the pompous look fell from his face for a moment as he turned to look blankly at Jack.

"What?" He murmured, his fat cheeks and flab oozed out from over the tight collar of his shirt jiggled like jelly.

"Look, I don't wish to be rude, but... I just want to sign want needs to be signed and get back home. I don't care what happens to the house. I won't be coming back here again."

Butterworth looked at him for a moment, he looked confused. Then after what felt like an eternity of silence between the two, Butterworth smiled.

"Well, then that is your prerogative. But none of it can be discussed out here in the street now can it?"

"No, I guess not."

"Good! Then shall we move on?"

The two carried on towards the office of Butterworth & Son, the sign was now visible at the end of the street.

CHAPTER 5

Jack stared at the silver horse head that topped Butterworth's cane as it leant up against the door in his compact office. Butterworth murmured obscenities as he searched the open drawer of the mahogany filling cabinet. Jack seemed transfixed by this horse head. The silver had been expertly engraved with every muscle and tendon present as he examined it from his seat near Butterworth's oversized pretentious desk, that seemed to dominate way too much of the room. His eyes squinted as he followed the slender but strong looking forehead that rounded out at its muzzle.

"Superb craftsmanship!" Jack murmured, his voice almost a whisper.

"Beg your pardon?" Butterworth said, his roundness turning on the spot, seeming to wobble a little.

"The cane... It's beautiful!"

"Ah, yes! Of course!" Butterworth grinned and slapped and large brown envelope onto the desk and then left it to approach the cane.

"It is magnificent isn't it?"

Jack nodded. As an artist himself he could appreciate such exquisite work. Butterworth picked up the cane. His chubby hand caressed the handle rubbing a plump thumb down the sleek contours of the horse's head, then followed the flow of its mane with his finger tips, until it changed from silver to a smooth beech shaft that had been lacquered in a classic black.

"It was actually a gift from your Grandfather!" Butterworth announced slapping the cane into the palm of his hand and ringing those chubby digits around it.

"Really?" Gasped Jack in awe.

"Yes, it was given to my Father many years ago. I've inherited it." He grinned, it was an arrogant grin, like the way a child would look at another child when it has something that the other desires, an almost spiteful smile.

"May I?" Jack asked holding out his hand.

"Oh! Yes, indeed!" Butterworth held out the cane towards Jack, the horse's head pointing at his face. Jack looked into its bright silver eyes that picked out the light from the bulb above them and sparkled. To Jack it seemed to wink at him as it moved, as if it knew secrets. Jack took the cane in his hands and he too examined it meticulously, not leaving any part of the handle unexplored. Butterworth stood watching for a moment, he looked almost jealous.

"Your Grandfather was a great man, I hope you know this?"

"Yeah, I remember." Was Jack's reply.

"Of course you do!" Butterworth smiled and returned to search for something in the filing cabinet.

"He actually helped my Father build this business you know?"

"Really?"

"Oh, yes! Mother used to say that they were thick as thieves." He chuckled, obviously a pleasant memory of his mother had manifested in his head.

"Obviously you know how your Grandfather came about his wealth?"

"Yeah! Horses."

"Not just horses my boy!" He scoffed, "Thoroughbreds! Race horses!"

"There's a difference?" Shrugged Jack.

"A huge difference!" Cried Butterworth spinning around from the filling cabinet drawer again.

"At the age of 18! Your Grandfather acquired his first horse in 1938 I believe it was? A stallion! Called Fosdyke, I believe your Grandfather acquired it from a farmer from somewhere in Lincolnshire. This was all much to the displeasure of your Great-Grandfather Kenneth I hear." He chuckled, his bulging torso resting against the cabinet drawer as he again laughed to himself and reminisced.

"Yeah, I remember hearing that he was a bit of a tyrant." Replied Jack, surprising himself that he did actually remember that.

"Too true my boy!" Butterworth chuckled, "He ruled his nest with a rod of iron, so I've heard. But anyway, I digress. This horse which he had purchased was affectionately called Red Admiral, due to its mahogany coloured coat. He proved an excellent stud indeed and won several races for your Grandfather."

"I think I remember..." Said Jack. Then his train of thought wandered away and an image of a reddish horse oil painting came into his mind's eye. Hanging on a wall, it was surrounded by an ostentatious gold gilded frame.

"Mr Heron? You were saying?" Asked Butterworth, easing back from his musing.

"Oh sorry, just reminiscing I guess!" He laughed, it was awkward as if he was embarrassed, "But, I think I remember a painting..."

"Hung on the wall of your Grandfather's study?" He smiled and nodded.

"Yes!"

"As did they all! All of your Grandfather's rosette winners made the wall. Must have been at least twenty of the buggers."

"24!" Jack answered quickly.

How did I know that? I remember! The wall of...

"Champions!" Jack bleated excitedly, "The wall of champions! That's what he called it!"

Jack was happy to be having some pleasant memories and thoughts enter his head. He could see the entire wall now, congested with all manner of framed paintings of all the winners his Grandfather had owned and trained.

"Yes, I can see them all now! Yellow Peril, Brown Cow, Blue Bottle! Oh and of course The Magic of Love!"

"Indeed!" Smiled Butterworth, "It is a sight to behold. There is only one horse that dons that wall that never won a rosette and that was that mischievous brute, Black Jack!"

The mention of the name 'Black Jack' sent a stabbing pain into Jack's head as though someone had skewered his skull with an icepick. He convulsed and dropped the cane onto the carpeted floor, while favouring his pulsating head. He saw a flash of the black horse and could have sworn that he had heard it neighing.

"Is everything alright, Mr Heron?" Gasped Butterworth as he came to his side quickly, not forgetting to pick up his cane as he did so.

"Yeah, I'm okay now." Jack winced, "It's just a headache that's all." He lied and rubbed at his temples.

"Can I get you anything? An aspirin? A glass of water perhaps?"

"No, no I'm okay now. Thank you." He forced a smile as his head throbbed.

"If you're sure?" Butterworth asked as he stood up and placed the cane back in its originally resting place. Jack nodded.

"Yes, he had huge success over the years in all manner of renowned competitions. Even a stint in World War II didn't harm his success. He sold off all his stallions before leaving for France, (With my Father I might add). I'd wager that they all went into farm work and the like, I doubt any of them ever saw a racetrack again. But he did keep a mare that he called 'Honeybutt' and she produced the next batch of champion studs for him on his return from the war."

Jack just nodded as he had no knowledge of this, he had no memory of his Grandfather ever talking about the war. He could only presume that his Grandfather was protecting him and such goings-on weren't meant for the ears of a young impressionable child. Or maybe the horrors that he had seen were too much for him to retell. Butterworth trudged back over to the filing cabinet and his head disappeared inside it, but he continued to talk.

"My Father helped him with the training of some of those horses and William gave a share of a huge National win one year that helped him set up this little business. So you could say we are indebted to your Grandfather and the Heron family for giving us a living."

The drawer was suddenly rammed in hard, out of sheer anger which made the whole room shudder.

"Where the bloody hell is it!" He sneered.

"Is everything okay, Mr Butterworth?" Jack asked, rising from his chair.

Butterworth turned to face him and smiled.

"Yes, yes, just can't seem to find a particular file that's all. Nothing to worry about."

Butterworth gestured for Jack to sit back down and he did the same on the other side of the desk. As he sat his wide load down on the chair it shrieked with pain, amazingly its wooden mortise and tenon joints held on, but it wasn't without the spasmodic groan with each movement of his portly buttocks.

"What file is missing?" Jack said already fearing the worst.

"It would appear that Patsy, that's my assistant, seems to have misplaced the deeds and paperwork that you need to sign for the family estate."

"Oh great!" He groaned, "Just great! Does that mean I'm stuck here?"

"Maybe for a few days I'm afraid." Butterworth's fat face contorted into an understanding face, but it did little to comfort an annoyed Jack.

"Patsy is away for the weekend visiting family in London. I will see if I can get in contact with her, but I have an important trip planned myself tomorrow as I'm off to Scotland on a matter of business and won't be back until Sunday."

"So I'm stuck here is what you are saying?"

"Until Sunday, yes I'm afraid so."

"Can't you just send me the files through on an email or through the post or something?"

"Unfortunately, no I'm afraid not. It was with the strict instructions in your Grandfather's Will that you must return here to sign them."

"Can we at least read the will?"

"Of course! Please try and calm yourself Mr Heron, I apologise for the missing file, I most solemnly do, but what can I do? It is but human error."

Jack exhaled and tried to calm himself down, he didn't wish to get so hot tempered, but the thought of staying here for a few days churned his stomach.

"I'm sorry for my outburst."

"Think nothing of it." Butterworth smiled again and opened up the envelope. Inside were several sheets of paper folded over and then sealed by a red wax stamp, the Heron family crest of a rearing horse behind a shield which had a large H on it, was embedded in the hardened wax.

"Had Grandad ever revised his will?"

"On a couple of occasions yes. After the death of your Mother and of course, your Auntie, he did have the will altered."

Pain shot through his head again, like the screaming high pitched cry of a bat had passed through him, leaving redness in its wake, cascading liquid the colour of crimson seemed to fall down his face blurring his vision.

"Mr Heron?" Butterworth asked, again he looked at him concerned.

"I'm fine." He nodded, "Just that headache again."
Butterworth clutched a paperknife from his desk and span the ivory handle around in his hand, the silver of the blade flashed at Jack. He broke the seal with ease and then opened up the last will and testament of William C. Heron. He perched some small spectacles on the end of his nose and held it up so that it was in a better position for him to read. He coughed a portly mans cough and began.

"I William Cyril Heron being of sound mind, do hereby bequeath the Heron House and the family estate to my Grandson, Jack Heron."
He nodded in acknowledgement to Jack and continued.

"Jack Heron will receive the full contents of Heron House and land, including the stables and five acres. As well as the £1,000,000.00 in bonds that will be in the secure hands of Butterworth & Sons, minus a 10% to Bertram Butterworth for all his and his Father's services over the years."

"So you get your cut, huh?" Jack scoffed.

"It's only natural, Mr Heron. I have gone to great lengths to tell you how indebted we are to your Grandfather, he obviously felt the same way about my family. But I assure you that 10% is the standard amount for what we do."

"Sorry, I didn't mean anything by it." Jack sighed.

"Not to worry." Butterworth grinned again.

"Can we just sell the house to someone who lives around here that might want to obtain it?"

"Oh no, Mr Heron, that won't be happening." Butterworth announced with almost humour in his voice.

"Why not? And what is so funny about that?"

"Nobody around here would dream of living in Heron House! Nobody around here would ever want too!"

"Why not?"

"Well, they are an old fashioned bunch around here. Superstitious you know."

"Superstitious?"

"With all that went on there. Nobody around here would touch it with a barge pole!"

Why are they superstitious? What went on there? Why can't I remember?

"Why? What happened?"

"Do you not remember?" Butterworth looked at him shocked.

"I...no! No, I don't?"

"W-well, I'm sure there will be someone from out of town that would love to get their hands on such a beautiful old building." Butterworth added trying to back peddle over what he had let slip out.   "Fin e. So, when you find the deeds, is there a way that I can just sign the house over to you? Then you can organise a sale and have a percentage of the final sale?"

"Oh yes, I'm sure we can accommodate such a proposal." Butterworth's smile widened across his plump face, it was the look of greed.

41

"Good! I don't want the house or anything in it."

"What about the bonds?" Butterworth queried.

"I'm a self-made millionaire, Mr Butterworth. I do not need my Grandfather's money. Give it to charity."

"That's very noble of you, Mr Heron, but unfortunately I can't do that. You have to sign for it and then it would have to be donated through the proper channels. I could..."

"Sort that out for a percentage no doubt." Jack intervened with a rolling of his eyes.

"Well, yes!" Butterworth replied almost embarrassed.

"You'll get it. So now what do I do? If I'm stuck her for a few days?"

"You could always scatter your Grandfather's ashes?" He said and with that he bent down and lifted up a large bronze urn with the initials W.C.H engraved on it, and rested it gently on the desk in front of Jack.

"He's been cremated already?" Jack asked in surprise.

"Yes, it was part of your Grandfather's wishes that he were cremated as soon as possible. He once said to me that the house had been so full of death that it smelt like death. He said he didn't want to add to that stench."

"Cheery!" Jack added staring at the urn.

"May I suggest a place for the scattering to take place?"

"Of course."

"The stables, I think would be fitting don't you?" He smiled a jolly smile and nodded his head. Jack agreed and scooped up the urn, its weight was surprising to him.

"Well, I guess I'd better find somewhere to stay. Is there a hotel around here?"

"There is only The Old Cock Inn, which is the local public house. They occasionally have rooms to let."

"Okay, I guess I'll try there then." Jack put out his hand and Butterworth eagerly shook it.

"So, I guess I shall see you on Sunday?"

"You will indeed. I have your cell number incase there is any change to the situation."

"Okay." Jack turned to leave.

"Oh, Mr Heron, there is another option."

Jack turned around to see Butterworth holding up the key to Heron House.

CHAPTER 6

Jack stood outside The Old Cock Inn. His bag clutched in his hand as the Welsh breeze caressed his mop of hair and sent it fluttering into disarray. He looked around the high street but there was no one around, not a soul joined him on those damp cobbles. He gazed curiously at the public house, the Tudor building was situated at the corner of the street. It stood firm and strong as though it were bearing the weight of all the other crooked houses on the street that seemed to lean on it for moral and physical support. It did not disappoint. Jack thought that if the pub gave up, then the entire row of houses would come crashing down like dominoes. He glanced around again, still it remained empty. Only a mist had joined him, snaking its way in through the dips in the hills in the distance and the sky had started to deepen, bringing with it a much darker tone. It was late afternoon now and this was one of the reasons why Jack was so surprised that he was standing alone on a street. Surely someone should be around?

Maybe they're all in the pub?

It seemed like a likely place to find country folk on a Friday afternoon, after they'd called it a day from their strenuous jobs in the farms and such. As the sky started to darken, the lights from the old pub seemed brighter, standing out on the high street like a beacon. The hanging sign moved rapidly all of a sudden, the metal brackets that held it intact squealed like hungry pigs. This startled Jack, who already felt on the verge of a mental breakdown. He glared up at the sign that swayed and squealed, swayed and squealed. The painting of a greying old cockerel seemed to mock him as it came into view and then out of view, as the wind pushed through it. Jack smiled knowing he was being silly to scowl at inanimate object and then stepped closer to take in the artwork. It was a lovely painting, but unfortunately the time and the weather had been unkind to the poor old cockerel, and it had not been maintained very well by the landlord.

I should give the landlord a piece of my mind, for neglecting such fine artwork as this.

He walked toward the public house and behind the door he could hear hearty conversation and joyous laughter. He breathed a sigh of relief as he had started to believe that Cyfrinach pwynt y De had become a ghost town. He pushed open the heavy wooden door and stepped inside. He was met by the warmth of the open fire, that was kicking up a frenzy in the stone hearth and there was a smell of stew cooking. To Jack, it smelt absolutely delicious and his stomach griped at him, reminding him that he had in fact not eaten since the plane and even that had only been a salad that he picked at. He had daren't eat too much for fear of being sick again. Unfortunately for Jack the warmth from the fire and the smell of stew was the only pleasantries he encountered on his arrival. The laughter had stopped, the conversations had stopped and all eyes had become fixated on this mysterious stranger that had just strolled in. He smiled and looked around. He met every face with his pleasant smile and was acknowledged with dubious scowls.

"Hello!" Jack squeaked and then swallowed hard. His Adam's apple seemed to fall down to his stomach, hit his intestines, causing his gut to grumble and croak embarrassingly, before ascending back up to his throat like a yoyo on a string. The locals slowly turned away to continue with their beer, stew or their card and domino games. But their conversations had become but a murmur, impossible for Jack to make out what was being said at any of the tables. If Jack was totally honest he would say that he didn't particularly wish to hear what was being said about him. His eyes caught the landlady. Her weathered face glared back at him untrusting, her chapped hands drying up a large glass tankard with a cloth. He smiled and approached the bar.

"Hello." He said pleasantly and placed his bag on a stool that was stood empty next to the bar. He was met with silence as she just wrinkled her nose at him and looked him up and down as if she were inspecting a mouldy piece of fruit she had discovered in the larder.

"I was wondering whether you had rooms to let?"
Still silence from the landlady and she turned her attentions back to cleaning the glass. Jack looked around, feeling a roomful of eyes burning holes into him. He felt anxious again, that kind of feeling you get when you have to stand up in class as a child and recite something from a book, or try to fathom a mathematical equation that you don't know the answer too.

"It would only be for a couple of nights." He stammered and spluttered, still trying to smile.
The landlady looked up from the glass and glared at him.

"We got no rooms." She snapped.

"Oh! I was told by Mr Butterworth that you may have…"

46

"Well," She interrupted, "you were told wrong, weren't ya." She groused matter of factly.

"Oh!" He sighed and looked around dejected and unwanted. He stood there for what seemed like the longest time, feeling as though any minute they would all explode from their chairs and linch him.

"Could I order some food?" He enquired, "That stew smells fabulous!"

"Stew's off!" She snapped and planted the tankard on the bar with such reckless abandon that she chipped a piece from its hefty base. Jack jumped again, he was so very jittery now.

"How about a drink?" He asked almost cringing, hoping that the tankard wouldn't find a new home on top of his head.

"What'd you want!" She snapped.

"Erm... A Scotch, please?" He smiled.

She poured him a Scotch and slammed it down on the bar. The amber coloured liquid lashed up the side of the small round glass and settled on the top of the bar.

"Thank you."

"Fiver!" She barked holding out her hand.

"Five pounds!" He said sounding a little shocked, "Is it a double?"

"You want it or not!" She growled.

"Yes, yes! A fiver is fine!" He said smiling as he delved into his expensive leather wallet that was spewing out notes of all value. He tried to conceal this from all the hawks that were watching, he thought that he might be mugged if they saw the contents. A smooth five pound note was pulled out and passed across, she snatched it with all the elegance of a bear trap.

"Watch my fingers." He quipped.

She stared at him with no humour in her face. Jack wondered whether her face had ever so much as cracked a smile. He thought that maybe it hadn't and he quickly scooped up the glass and his bag, and moved to the corner of the room where there was a free table. He left behind him a trail of Scotch droplets that fell from the base of the glass.

Wow! So much for a warm homecoming! He thought as he sat down and tried not to make eye contact with anyone.

As he sat alone sipping at his Scotch, he took out the key to Heron House and examined it. A black cast iron key lay in the palm of his hand, it was heavier than he had expected. He rubbed his fingertips over the rugged bit, its teeth were sharp with splintering metal. Then working his way up its long slender stem he found the roundness of its collar and then circled to the bow, which was smooth to the touch. The design within the bow of the key displayed that Heron family crest again. When his fingertips touched that black rearing stallion, he felt another flash within his minds eye and saw the snorting fury of a black horse's nostrils and then it was gone. Vomit rose up again and fizzed around his throat before descending.

What the fucking hell is wrong with me? What the fuck is wrong with this place!

He discarded the key onto the worn sticky table which was topped with a hundred rings from tankards past. He dove into his pocket for his cell phone.

Marcy! I need to call Marcy and tell her... Tell her what exactly?

48

He touched the screen and it illuminated the dimly lit corner in which he sat. A photograph of himself and Marcy standing outside the new gallery greeted him and that made him smile. It made him feel normal, safe. The battery was running at 60% and there was no signal at all.

"Damn it! I'm stranded out here!" He sighed. He had another drink and looking up he noticed an old woman in the other corner. She looked ancient and haggard, her skin hanging from her withered face and she smiled an almost toothless smile at him. He instinctively recoiled and then presumed that that may have come across as very rude, so he forced a smile and a nod. She rose from her chair and started to shuffle towards him. Grey greasy hair cascaded down either side of her languished narrow face. Hair sprouted at random from her nose, chin and above her upper lip. She used a walking stick to help her make her way to Jack, slowly and methodically.

Oh my God! She looks like a witch! The witch from Hansel and Gretel! She's coming for me!

He imagined himself gulping down the remainder of his drink and making a sharp exit for the door, but then he thought that would be incredibly rude as she was the first friendly face he had seen in this place and should really give her the benefit of the doubt. She lowered herself into the chair opposite him very slowly. Jack thought of her movements as lackadaisical as a stair lift.

"Hello, my boy!" She said, as she sat with a sigh.

"Hello, there Miss..." He waited for her to introduce herself and a crazy thought entered his head.

Oh please say your name is Patsy! Please say it is! You've found the deeds and I can sign them and be gone from this place.

"Crowfoot, Mrs Crowfoot!" She smiled showing off the few little teeth that she did have, that sprouted out of her gums like sloping gravestones.

"Pleased to meet you." Jack said with a smile, "Can I buy you a drink?" He offered almost rising to go back to the bar.

"Oh, no! I don't drink alcohol. Nasty bloody stuff! Did my brother Sidney in, did the drink you know? Yes, ravaged his liver something rotten it did!"

"Sorry to hear that." He said sitting back down. "Everything in moderation I guess."

"Indeed."

"And what is your name? What brings you to these parts?" She enquired.

"Oh I am sorry! How rude of me! My name is Jack. Jack Heron." There was almost an unanimous gasp from the room that seemed to suck all the air out of the place. Some people actually got up and left in such a hurry that they left drinks half drunk and stews half eaten.

"Heron!" The landlady caterwauled, "Get him out of here!"
Some burly men actually stood and looked as they were approaching him to literally throw him out.

"Joanie!" Shouted Mrs Crowfoot, "Shut your squealing! Leave the boy alone and mind your business!"
The two men backed off and returned to their seats. The landlady disappeared into the back room. Mrs Crowfoot turned back and

50

stared at him. Her eyes were wise and kind, a blue, grey pastel that made him feel safe.

"Heron, you say?" She said glancing down at the key.

"I see."

"Have I done something wrong coming here?"

"No, no of course not! They're just a superstitious bunch."

"Superstitious?" Jack murmured, remembering that Mr Butterworth had said the same thing to him earlier on.

"The old man died you know? Were you a relation?"

"Erm, yes, I'm his... William's Grandson."

She seemed to ponder this for a moment.

"Ah! You're the one that escaped aren't you?"

"Escaped? Well, I left..."

"Same thing!" She sniffed dismissively as wet mucus slipped back up her nostril.

"I left when I was 16 to attend art colleague in London."

"Good for you!" She grinned, "And now you've come back. You've missed the funeral you know?"

"I know." Jack said sadly, he had started to feel very sentimental about his Grandfather. Just being here made warming memories and thoughts come back to him of how nice his Grandfather was.

"You're not thinking of going up to the house though are you? I wouldn't if I was you. Just say your goodbyes to your Granddaddy and head on back home. There's nothing for you up there but heartache."

"But, what do you mean?"

51

"Bad things happened in that house. Very bad things! I'd avoid the place at all costs!"

"What bad things?" Jack pleaded and suddenly felt a layer of sweat build up on his brow.

"I guess you were too young to remember such goings on. Maybe they shielded you from what happened."

"What things!" He pleaded. But she didn't hear his petitioning.

"It's no wonder that he became a recluse! The silly old sod was probably scared to come out and face the public after what went on." Jack looked at her confused and now sweating profusely.

"But, William was a good man, he would have hidden such horrors from young eyes. You would have been too young to understand such pain."

"What are you talking about!" He finally screamed, banging his fists on the table, causing the remains of his Scotch to be whipped into a frenzy at the bottom of the glass. Everyone stared at him, some eyes even appeared scared of him.

"Right, that's enough! Get him bloody out of here!" The landlady shouted as she appeared at the bar again and with that announcement a number of burly men stood up again.

"Oh, will you shut up, Joanie!"

She disappeared again in a huff, this time the burly men remained standing. Mrs Crowfoot leaned back in her chair and gazed at him.

"Maybe you did see. Maybe you have seen the horrors."

"What horrors? I don't know what you're talking about!" His eyes now bloodshot and holding back tears of frustration, his hair thick with sweat falling in front his face. She leaned in very close to

Jack, whose heart rate had suddenly seemed to skyrocket out of control. Her hair now almost touching his as she stared into his worried eyes.

"Maybe you do need to go back to that house. Maybe you do need to see it again."

"See what again?" He whispered.

She held the key up between them his eyes flitted back and forth from her eyes and the key, before she thrust it at him.

"That's for your eyes only Jack." She whispered as Jack reluctantly took the key.

CHAPTER 7

It was dark by the time Jack arrived at the gates of the Heron House estate. He'd managed to thumb a lift on the back of a hay cart that was trundling along the road. While on the dilapidated old excuse for a cart, he thought that he could probably get to where he was going quicker on foot, but he was tired and fed up although confused more than anything.

The driver of the cart had remained mute on the journey, but Jack wasn't about to do himself out of a free ride by opening his mouth again, so he enjoyed the quiet. The driver had stopped outside the gates and refused to go any further. It was at least half a mile walk up the gravelled drive to where the house stood. Jack had tried to tip the driver but he had ignored him and trundled away into the darkness along a dirt road.

Jack cradled his Grandfather's urn under his arm as he looked up at the cast iron gates, the initials H and H crafted into the design. It looked as though it had not been looked after at all. The majority of its black paint had long since peeled off, unveiling the unprotected parts to succumb to rust. Vines had also grown upon them, wrapping themselves around the weary bars relentlessly, spitefully claiming the gate as its own, clutching it tightly and unwilling to share. Jack grabbed his bag and pushed open the gate that screamed like a wounded child, the hinges grinding unpleasantly in Jack's ears. He stopped pushing when the gap was big enough for him to pass through, he could no longer stand to listen to such misery. In the dark sky he couldn't make out where the house actually was, so he followed the gravel driveway that lead the way. Part of him hoped that the house would be gone when he got there. The other part felt like throwing up.

CHAPTER 8

Jack trudged up the driveway to the house with only the crushing of stones underfoot and the occasionally hooting of a distant owl for company. It was so dark now that he was moving on instinct alone. Every so often the breeze would move the clouds on long enough for the moon to emerge, bathing the Welsh countryside in its ivory glow, before being swallowed up and consumed again by the mass of clouds. To Jack those clouds looked like trouble.

Maybe there's a storm on the way?

His thoughts did not deceive him. There was indeed a storm on its way, the distant rumblings had already started to manifest in Jacks mind, body and even soul. He walked slowly and tentatively, when you would have thought that a man with a thin jacket, strolling through the blistery Welsh countryside at night would have been raring to reach his destination. There was something that held him back from quickening his pace. That sickening feeling in the pit of his stomach had reared its ugly head. His heart rate had increased and there was a layer of tacky sweat that clung to his flesh. It was the kind of sensation you get when you're wrapped up in bed with a fever. The moon appeared again and he was immediately halted in a cold numbing sensation. That sensation was fear. The moons beam lit up the gigantic Victorian mansion that stood no more than 20 feet away from the shivering, perspiring mess that had replaced Jack

Heron. He felt like he had all of a sudden been sucked back through some portal of time. He felt as though he was shrinking, like he was a child again. He envisioned himself standing there in the glow of the moon, eyes like saucers as they fixated on the house, but he was indeed a child. Shrunken and draped in his grown up clothes, clinging on to a bag that was as big as him. The breeze blew through him and he shivered, stirring him from his woolgathering as he fixed his glare on the house again. The dark structure of sandstone rose out of the ground and stood defiantly. Time had not been kind to the house that Jack's Great-Grandfather had built on his initial fortune made from Heron's Biscuits. It had been constructed when Queen Victoria still sat on the throne and had only ever had two owners, technically three now. The feelings stirred within Jack again tugging away at his internal organs like he was some puppet on strings being controlled. He staggered closer to the house, stagger because a part of him was trying with all its might to stay where he was, but to no avail. His smart leather shoes shuffled through the gravel, caking them in a layer of dust. His neck was forced back as he grew closer, arching back as far as his pleading spine would allow. He looked like a tourist on their first trip to a major city, who get captivated by the awing allure of such gargantuan architecture. He felt as though his neck would snap at any minute as he gawked up at the building. Jagged gothic shards that protruded from it as though they were the canines of some diabolical vampire, looking to sink those fragments into the softness of the moon and feed. The moon was gone again and now he found himself at the entrance of Heron House. His body now physically shook convulsions through his entire body, as his eyes found the door. In the darkness it appeared to him to be brown in colour, almost dirty, paint peeling from it like the skin of a leper. It was then that he saw the knocker, the cast iron rearing of a black stallion.

"Black Jack!" He murmured, his voice shaking as much as his slender frame. He had seen this door before, of course he had in his past when he was a child everyday, but no that wasn't it. He had seen this door a few days ago. He dropped the bag onto the steps. One hand still hugging the urn tightly to his chest as his other hand disappeared into his coat pocket retrieving the key. He held it up to the door in front of him. The horse on the bow of the key matched the knocker perfectly. Apart from the Heron crest it was exactly the same. Somewhere he heard the distance neighing of a horse.

"The door! Oh my God the door! It's my door... My piece in the gallery! It's my door!" The words spilled out in terror. He shook with disbelief and then felt the urge to vomit. He collapsed to his knees and threw up, it was water the colour of amber whiskey, but in the darkness it appeared like everything else to him, black. He clutched the urn tightly as if for some kind of security or reassurance as he plucked up the courage to face the door. It appeared to stand over him, mocking him as he wiped the vomit from his lips and scowled.

"Enjoying this aren't you, you fuck!" He growled as he rose to his feet.

"You want me? You got me!" And with that statement, he charged towards the door and slotted the key into the lock. It slipped in easily and came together as naturally as male and female reproductive organs. He turned the key which crunched angrily as it

58

opened. The large hallway stood silent in darkness. Jack grabbed his bag and strode inside slamming the door behind him.

"Right!" He bellowed in frustration, "You've got me here! Now what?"

The faces in his dream flashed before him again rapidly, causing him to scream in pain and drop to his knees. He clung to the urn as the lid rattled uncontrollably, somehow managing to stay in place and waited for those faces to disappear once again. As he panted trying to catch his breath, the knocker shook and rattled against the door which was still trembling from the force that he had slammed it.

Rat-a-tat-tat.

Rat-a-tat-tat.

Rat-a-tat.

Rat-a.

Rat.

CHAPTER 9

Jack stood in the cold narrow hallway for the longest time. It seemed like he had caught the gaze of the gorgon herself, Medusa, and had been preserved in stone for eternity. The wind kicked up a fuss outside and seemed to whip the door knocker into a frenzy again, always with that Rat-a-tat-tat, Rat-a-tat-tat that felt oh so familiar to him. He gripped the urn to his chest for dear life and felt as though he had been holding his breath, as if paralysed by shock. Those thoughts, memories or visions of a past he could not quite remember, hurtled through his mind rapidly slicing through his brain and causing him piercing pain as these images manifested before him. When finally, he exhaled and the warm vapour rose up and attacked the cold house. At the sight of this, Jack shuddered. A layer of gooseflesh caressed his skin, feeling like thousands of tiny insects were squirming all over him causing him to shudder again. The fog of warming breath had evaporated and he dropped his bag to the cold tiled floor. The sudden sound echoed around the hallway and up the large staircase in front of him, reverberating in the darkness that awaited on the next floor. Jack quickly flicked on the ageing light switch. The light erupted from teardrop shaped bulbs that sat tightly in an extravagant golden chandelier, which had unfortunately become consumed by a thick layer of dust. One of the bulbs popped and the others seemed to pulse on and off before settling and finally, the hallway was illuminated. The urn shook in his quivering grip, its lid reverberating up and down rapidly. Finally he gently placed it down on the cabinet in the hallway and sighed with relief. He was terrified he would drop it and lose the contents. He looked down at the floor of the hallway. The tiles were in an exquisite original design, a feature that was as old as the house itself. Tiny diamonds joined together like the scales of a lizards. This original feature that had never been altered or vulgarly covered by carpets or rugs, was left to breathe and flaunt its refinement. Jack remembered this tiled floor. A sensation pricked at his toes like bee stings as he remembered running across this floor barefoot as a youngster. The cold tiles causing him to hop and skip quickly into a room that had been graced with carpet. He smiled at this but then glanced up the stairs into the darkness that appeared dense, a thick blackness that would surely consume him if he were to enter. He glanced around the hallway, not a lot had changed, he seemed to sense that much. He made a point of ignoring the darkness of the stairs and stared down the corridor that lead to a sitting room and then the kitchen. To his right, thick mahogany double doors homed the dining room. They had been left ajar and Jack not wanting to move, craned his neck to peek inside. It sat in darkness as did a gigantic oval table now unused and unloved, left to cower like some flea bitten dog. In happier times, long ago it would have been surrounded by a family of seven enjoying the modesty of the family's wealth and indulging in routine five course meals. When the warmth of such memories smudged and became dark, he turned away. His attentions now to his lefthand side and the other room, the doors open and inviting to his Grandfather's study. He forced his legs to move and carry his anxious carcass towards the room where he entered and flicked on the light. The study filled him with a thawing feeling, loving and caring that seemed to make him feel safe. He remembered the large mahogany desk and creaky chair that was positioned in front of the long oblong windows. They were leaded and looked out onto the fields that bled out from the stables on the hill, although neither fields nor stables could be seen in the pitch black of the night. The large majestic fireplace sat cold, but with the remains of an old fire which would have been burning a few days ago while his Grandfather fought death. No doubt sat in his worn olive green, wingback Chesterfield armchair. The chair that still had the curvatures of his Grandfather's buttocks sunk into the cracked leather and foam of the seat. Jack approached the chair and rubbed a hand across the back of it feeling all the cracks in the leather that ran away in all directions, giving it the appearance of country lanes on a road map.

"I definitely remember this old boy." Said Jack and he smiled fondly.

He looked above the mantel and gazed at the large oil painting of his Grandfather. A portrait of him holding the reigns of Honeybutt, his Grandfather's personal favourite mare.

"Grandad!" Jack whimpered and his eyes welled up with moisture. Tears slowly emerged from behind his eyelids and then rolled over his high cheekbones before picking up speed and cascading down his gaunt face. Tears conceived out of sorrow, pain and embarrassment. He felt ashamed that he could not remember his Grandfather's face up until this point, until actually seeing his face in the painting. A face that resembled Jack immensely, the thin face, floppy hair and pointed chin, even their narrow smiles were similar. Although his grandfather's happened to be wrapped with a bushy grey moustache.

"I'm so sorry, Grandad," He sighed and collapsed into the armchair, uncontrollably sobbing into his hands.

"I am so very sorry that I forgot you."

His sniffling begged for forgiveness, but unfortunately the acceptance of such a proposal could never be answered.

CHAPTER 10

Jack had managed to get a fire started and immediately the fire did its job and warmed up the room nicely. He had found the drinks cabinet and had poured himself a very large Scotch, believing that he well and truly needed it. Jack had put off any thought of venturing further into the house, he couldn't stand too much reminiscing at one time.

He had managed to push those haunting thoughts and mental apparitions to the back of his mind and instead, focused his attentions on his Grandfather's 'Wall of Champions'. He had even managed to ignore the several thumps that he had heard coming from upstairs, he could not deal with such a thought that he was not alone in the house. He simply pretended that it hadn't happened, a trait that he had become remarkable at over the last twenty years. The wall of faded green wallpaper was inundated with rectangles of golden guilt. Each one homed a different horse that had been trained by his Grandfather and had gone on to make him very proud by attaining so many accolades and championships throughout the years, as well as making him a very rich man indeed. Jack smiled as he sipped his Grandfather's ageing Scotch and studied the paintings of the horses that had helped produce The Heron family fortune.

"In a way, I suppose I owe all my success to you." He chuckled and held his glass up to the stallions and fillies that congested the wall, as if making a toast to them. He remembered some of them now, some had still been around when Jack was a boy, when his Grandfather was still involved in the racing business. The majority of them had been before his time, but he remembered fondly that his Grandfather would hoist him up into his arms and he would tell him stories about each horse, what races they had won or what their temperaments had been like. He had held them all in high regard as they had all served him well. Jack had often worried about where the bodies of the old horses had gone when they had died. Had they gone to the glue factory like tales that he had heard when he was just knee high to a grasshopper, or had they been buried somewhere on the grounds? Jack theorised this question now in his adulthood and presumed it to be the latter. There was another thump which came from above. The ceiling reverberated and Jack stopped mid sip and his eyes rolled upwards to glare fearfully at the ceiling. Cobwebs were stretched out across the ceiling and even a tiny little spider scuttled away and fled to safety from the loud thud from above. He swallowed the Scotch hard and again, dark deeds flashed in his head, like jigsaw pieces made from razorblades, slicing away at his grey matter. Still he tried to form the completed puzzle, but his mind would not allow it. His stomach gurgled as if cooking up another batch of vomit porridge. His heart rapidly beating again as his lungs acted like two ends of a vice, squeezing firmly, tightly sandwiching his heart. The tight chested feeling of anxiety had started to consume his whole body and breaths seemed hard to come by. The feeling was indescribable. It was as if his whole ribcage was compressing, crushing his internal organs until they burst and become nothing more than pulpy chunks of viscera. But on the other side of the coin it simultaneously felt like his whole torso was going to explode. As if his organs were expanded with the aim to burst out from him and smother those splendid paintings with his innards. He felt like he had imagined this happening and then blinked as a shaking hand manoeuvred the glass of Scotch back to his lips. In such a quivering motion the rim of the glass clipped his teeth and caused him to wince. He managed to swallow almost all of the contents and then stared at the paintings again, looking to those champions of the past for help or guidance.

"Make it go away." He whispered.

Then he thought of something he hadn't thought of in a long time, the reason being that he hadn't needed to do such a thing for years.

"Suppress it!" He murmured, "Lock it up, hide it, suppress it!" A technique he had used in the past to escape these feelings and thoughts, these hauntings. He would concentrate on something he loved, thinking of something that he held dear or made him happy. A nostalgic feeling perhaps that held pleasant memories for him that he could focus on. A light that could cut through the darkness that consumed him. But what could he focus on?

"The horses!" He blurted irrationally.

He started to turn his attentions to the paintings on the wall, focusing on each one and remembering what his Grandfather had told him about them. He could feel the loving protective cradle that came by being swaddled by his Grandfather's arms. They were strong arms, working mans arms. Although he had made his fortune racing horses, he had still broke his back laying the foundations for such a venture. Building the stables, rearing the horses, caring for them, mucking them out and teaching them. He could still feel those fears that seemed to be tearing away at him internally so he began to name the horses and what colours they were. He remembered now that that was how he learnt his colours when he was very young. He learnt most of the colours through the horses and learnt the terminology of the various colours.

"Red Admiral was sorrel. Blue Bottle, iron grey. Fosdyke, chestnut. Honeybutt, yellow, well, blonde, she was a Palomino. The Magic of Love, silver, well grey really, Cremellis. Such a beautiful luscious shimmering mane!"

He had started to calm now and the suppression seemed to be doing its job.

"Brown Cow was dark bay." He continued not shivering at all now and completely focused at the task in hand.

"Yellow Peril, a sand coloured Appaloosa. Sir Rodney, a Roan, yes! A Strawberry Roan! Oakley! He came from America I remember! A large Tobian colt! Gladstone, light bay as was his brother Khasi."   H   e
seemed very relaxed and calm now and continued to say the horses names in his head as he moved over to the fireplace and again sat in his Grandfather's chair.

Tinkle, Maj (short for Majesty), Paradise (She was gorgeous grey, almost blue in some lights), Bumble, Bliss and Fancey.

He could hear the wind outside and whistling around the chimney, the flames fluttered in the fireplace. He stoked it a little, forcing it into life again and leant back in the chair and continued to sip at his drink, still remembering those horses.

Dimple, Peg, Slobottom (Grandad said he was a slow old bugger,
managed a few rosettes though. Rough Diamond,
Marjoribanks and Zig Zig.

He smiled to himself as his eyelids flickered wearily. The wind howling and the leather creaking under his movements were the only sounds in the house now and he felt perfectly at peace. Then it was as if that little devil on his shoulder whispered in his ear, its forked tongue wriggling away spurting poison. It left the name of the one horse that Jack had forgotten about or chosen to ignore. Granted it shouldn't have been included on 'The Wall of Champions' but it was still there. Standing an incredible 18 hands high, black as pitch and as menacing as a hungry tiger, he wasn't fit for competition. Too unpredictable too aggressive.

"Black Jack!" He cried and gulped at the same time. He scrambled out of the chair and towards the decanter holding that rich and comforting Scotch. He poured himself another full glass and spilled it quite a lot before dashing backwards to the chair and collapsing into it once again. He stared at the dancing flames and again tried to forget the anxiety, forget the fear, the fear of Black Jack. He closed his eyes dreamily and began to recite all the horses again.

CHAPTER 11

Jack felt like a child again as he crept up the stairs and into the dark mouth of nothingness. He gazed down at his feet that were now bare. Each stair creaked under his reluctant steps, each one of them generating a different sound, like he was tiptoeing across the keys of an enormous piano. He arrived at the top of the stairs and shuffled forward onto the landing that seemed to go on without end. There was nothing but darkness and he wondered why on earth he had not thought to bring a light with him, but still he moved on. The soles of his feet caressing the soft comfortable carpet with each tentative step.

Thump! Thump! Thump!

The sound came loud and erratically. It was enough to halt him mid stride and he waited, listening, part of him hoping that it would not happen again.

"I must go on." The sound had stopped again and he moved along the dark corridor searching for the room that the sound was coming from, but in truth he knew exactly which room it was.

Thump! Crash! Thump!

He stopped in his tracks again. His breathing pattern had changed now and his chest moved up and down rapidly. In his head the sound of the constant wheezing breaths felt detached, like it wasn't even him making that petrified whine.

Crash! Smash! Thump!

A cacophony blared angrily from behind a door that he now found himself situated in front of. He thought he had heard a high pitch shriek escape underneath the door after the last outcry, but he could not be certain for sure. Maybe he had imagined the wailing? He hoped for his own sanity that he had imagined it. He balled a fist on an outstretched arm as if to knock the door, but it just hovered out in front of him, appearing tiny and far away. The urge to knock the door was strong, like a feeling of familiarity, but something was holding him back from going through with it. But what could be holding him back? Fear. Fear was what had brought him to a standstill, it seemed to grasp his larynx firmly in its sadistic vice, evidently holding oxygen for ransom.

Thump! Crash! Smash! Bang!

The onslaught came again and his quivering hand recoiled and hung by his side. It remained balled up in a tight and clammy fist, swaying gently like a pendulum in the damp cold breeze, that he could feel working its way from underneath the door.

A light flickered and then came on from behind the door. The carpet where he stood was now illuminated. He saw his toenails gleam in its brightness, his feet looked small and far away too. His head now felt fuzzy and confused.

There's someone in there! The words exploded in his head, aggressively and boisterous like the distressing howl of an air raid siren.

Get the fuck out of here! There's someone in there!

He panicked and started to sweat profusely, his whole body felt clammy, his skin hot and sticky.

70

Get out! Get out! Get out! Wailed in his head, he thought that at any moment his head would actually explode and the words would fall to the floor and scuttle away. Still he stood rooted in front of the door, bare-feet close together, surrounded in a square of the brightest ivory.

Get out! Are the words that echoed through his head repeatedly. Still he stood there, frozen. A part of him wanted to shake himself hard by the shoulders or slap his face and tell him to move himself, but he didn't move, couldn't move.

"Get out!" Came the shriek that rose from under the door and smothered him like a shroud. He shivered and shook like a flag on a mast, that did not come from his head. It was almost safe inside his head, where his own thoughts played tricks and games with him, that was okay wasn't it? That was manageable, that type of behaviour could be deduced and pigeonholed as '*Mind playing tricks on me.*' But when that same trick was now being played on another board, this time outside the safety of his subconscious then all bets were off.

"Get out! Get out! Get out!" Came the constant shrieking from the room. Then without warning it stopped. There was nothingness again, he heard the sound of rain outside, but loudly and the wind whistling around the house. He exhaled and a shudder tiptoed down his spine as he did so.

"It's all in your head, Jack!" He finally told himself aloud and reached for the door knob, he stopped for a moment as he caught his reflection in the brass and frowned. He looked so young in the reflection, like he was staring at a sepia photograph from the past, his past. He leaned in and saw that it was a trick of the light and just his tired, gaunt and scared face staring back at him.

"This is ridiculous!" Jack said and opened the door.

A bed chamber stood in disarray. The large four poster bed had taken up most of the room and the curtains that hung from its frame and attached around the bulky spindles with matching tiebacks fluttered, as if trying to escape its confines. It was then that he noticed the thick burgundy curtains drifting towards him on a consistent gust from an open window. Jack breathed a sigh of relief and then noticed a number of items that had been knocked from a dresser that sat below the window.

"See! I knew there would be a rational explanation for all of this!" He said trying to convince himself that he hadn't at all been scared and he knew all along what the outcome would be when he opened the door. As he stepped forward he trod on something sharp which carved its way into the sole of his foot.

"Oh! Shit!" He seethed and looked down to see broken perfume bottles everywhere. He lifted up his foot and picked out the shard of broken glass that protruded from his flesh and watched as blood trickled from the wound. It was not a deep laceration and did not really hurt him if truth be told, but a part of him felt like crying. He wanted to sob uncontrollably, like a child. He told himself that it may be that there was a trace of the perfume on the glass that had caused the wound to sting.

"Bloody perfume!" He stopped wincing for a moment and thought, "Mums perfume?"

He smelt the air, inhaling deeply. It was as if it had been freshly sprayed into the air.

"Mums room!" He remembered dreamily.

In a daze he suddenly looked up from his foot and saw something hurtle towards him from behind the flailing curtains. A mourning apparition dressed head to toe in black. No, there were no toes! It seemed to be floating, defying gravity in a way that no living human being could. It screamed at him furiously.

"I said get out!" It wailed. The turbulent gale from behind it added emphasis to the enraged war cry of this banshee. Its face was hidden behind a black veil but on closer inspection there was seemingly no face, only a hole where a face should have been. The hole was large and deep, crooked teeth like protrusions bulged out from around its edges in random fashion. Spittle sprayed out in all directions, drenching the inside of the black lace veil that concealed the horrid pit of emptiness. It screamed furiously for Jack to leave, its hatred spewing out constantly. Jack screamed and teetered backwards towards the door, bouncing off the door frame. It seemed to soar towards him with great speed and velocity,. The long black gown of lace it wore quivering in its wake. Jack screamed again and fell back onto the landing unceremoniously on his backside helplessly. The harpy seemed to consume the doorway and then the door slammed shut and the light went out. Darkness. Nothingness.

Jack fell out of his Grandfather's chair in the study, sweating profusely in front of the raging fire. He found himself on all fours and breathing heavily. He stared into the flames and then looked around the room. Regaining his composure and familiarising himself with his whereabouts, he suddenly started to laugh. It was a nervous laugh at first, but then quickly manifested into a relieved snicker.

73

"Only a bloody dream, you idiot!" He told himself as he climbed back into his seat.

"Ow!" He winced and as he sat, he looked down at his feet that for some reason were bare. "What the..." He asked himself before trailing off without finishing his question. As he turned his foot around he saw a small incision. A trickling of blood oozing from it caused his heart to skip and his mouth to gape.

Get out! Came the ghostly whisper somewhere in his head, or was it in his head?

Thump! Thump! Thump!

Came the commotion from upstairs again, slowly he looked up staring wide eyed at the ceiling.

Thump! Thump! Thump!

CHAPTER 12

Jack had somehow pushed aside the disturbing sound of that unrelenting ruckus that continued to besiege the room above him. The copious amounts of his Grandfather's Scotch that he had decimated in the last hour or so, had helped to drown it out. The bulbous clouds outside had brought with them rain and slowly it had started to fall, immediately it was swept up by the vicious wind and spat out in all directions. The dark sky threatened thunder but at this moment in time, Jack could not care less what the weather was doing, he had started to drink heavily. He may have been drinking to forget what he had seen, or what he had thought he had witnessed or indeed possibly dreamt. He drank to block out the commotion that was going on above, and those dark visions of memory. He drank to ignore the whistling gale that had surrounded Heron House, hissing its spiteful whisper through the cracks in the old building's mortar. It would appear that he was drinking so much he would eventually pass out and then he would not have to deal with any of it, especially the constant Rat-a-tat-tat of the door knocker that would not quit. It was as if some stubborn door to door salesman refused to leave until he had said his piece. He staggered and stumbled across the study to the bar and found that the crystal cut glass decanter was now empty. In his drunken haze, he removed the stopper and held it upside down watching as a few remaining drops escaped its confines.

75

"Oh, Sod it!" He garbled, dribbling as he swayed from side to side on the spot, as if that blusterous gale that was building outside was responsible. He unceremoniously set the decanter back on the bar top and continued to drink nothingness from the empty glass.

"Guess I'd better get another bottle of your finest Granddaddy." He slurred.

He zigzagged across the room again. One hand still clutching his empty glass, the other reaching out to grab hold of random pieces of furniture to keep him upright, as he made his arduous journey to the desk.

"Gotta call someone and get out of here!" He suddenly announced sounding very sober, as if it was the scared voice of Jack Heron, deep from within making the plea. Jack reached the desk and collapsed on top of it, his arms stretching out towards his cell phone that seemed miles away from his grasp. He looked at the phone through blurred vision and fluttering eyelids. His finger touched the screen and it burst into life. The light of the screen illuminating its surroundings. He managed to grab it and bring it so very close to his face. He tried to focus on the screen, there is still no signal, and the battery is now running at 39%. He lets go of it and it drops to the top of the table and Jack's eyelids quiver rapidly as if he had suddenly sunk into the middle of a dreamlike state. There was silence, finally. The shock of the sudden silence caused Jack to open up an eye again. It swirled around in its socket surveying the gloomily lit room before being safely nestled away again behind his eyelid. Then came the dripping. The dripping of water. In his minds eye he saw a tap, its reflective carbon steel structure trying with all its might to gleam, but being unable to because of the thick layer of moisture that had devoured it. Droplets formed and fell from its spout, each one colliding with the unforgiving cast iron bath that he suddenly felt himself in, cold against his naked flesh. But surely this could not be? Jack Heron lay unconscious on the worn maroon carpet of his Grandfather's study, did he not? Each droplet that fell sounded like a gunshot erupting in his head. Faster and faster the drops fell, each one feeling like a needle piercing his brain. Quickly it manifested into a constant torrential flurry as if the tap had been loosened to release the chilly water within. The water started to surround him in a cold cast iron coffin, his body limp and lifeless, unable to escape this uncomfortable wash routine. Under the vigorous flow of cold water, his body suddenly erupted in a layer of gooseflesh and underneath his skin, his body shivered. The water suddenly stopped and the spout seemed to cough and splutter, dealing with a liquid that was maybe too thick for it to regurgitate. However it managed to do so and that is when Jack started to feel the warmth. On his toes at first, droplets of thick red blood started to cover them and then seep into the water filling the bath with its hot tacky substance. Its warmth was enough to cure Jack's sudden case of gooseflesh, but when the realisation crept in of what this substance was, he suddenly became overwhelmed. The blood flowed out of the spout relentlessly over and over again, starting to smother him. He could take no more. Jack screamed and slid off the table onto the floor. He could still hear the droplets falling, falling like rain. He turned to face the large leaded window and watched as the raindrops fell on the other side of the glass and thudded forcefully on the windowsill. His breathing quivered and he let out a heavy sigh of relief.

CHAPTER 13

Jack was woken suddenly by the clamour of the old Grandfather clock that stood forgotten in the hall. The clocks hidden duo of the dusty hammer and rusting bell worked in unison to bring the house back to life as it struck. Jack peeled himself off the carpet where he had lain for an hour or so in a moist puddle of drool. His eyes flickered and tried to focus as the chiming of the clock shook his aching head. He sat up and leant against the desk rubbing at his head each time the hammer pounded against its bell.

"Okay, okay! Give it a rest already!" He moaned, but still the clock chimed, not willing to concede until its task had been accomplished.

"What an awful bloody din!" He groaned and wondered to himself why the clock had only just started to strike. It rang and rang and rang.

"Knock it off!" He shouted.

Suddenly it stopped. Jack may have thought for moment that he had been responsible for the halting of the chime, but in fact the mechanism had finished its task.

"Good!" Jack scoffed and pulled himself up by the desk and sat on it, working the sleep out of the corner of his eyes with his fingertips. He looked out at the open door to the hallway where he could see the clock. He hadn't even heard the ticking if he had been honest and staring at it now he could hear nothing. He seemed transfixed by it, the pendulum did not swing, it did not tick. Even watching it for several minutes did not urge the minute hand around its face. The sudden unexpected wake up call seemed to sober him up a little.

"It's broken." He said to himself in some confusion, "Then how did it chime?"

A shudder fingered his spinal column like a pianist tinkering the ivories of a grand piano. He could have spent more time pondering this curious occurrence, but he was interrupted by the churning of his empty stomach and realised he still hadn't eaten.

"I best brave it and go and see if there is anything in the kitchen." He stuttered as he glared into the open hallway.

That anxiety started to tighten around his chest again, and the paranoia of what could be waiting for him out there chipped away at him.

"Enough!" He shouted sternly and stood up, rather too quickly and his head spun and nearly saw him collapse onto the desk again. He managed to steady himself and then grabbed his cell phone. The time read 00:07 now, he glanced at his battery (now at 28%) and growled at the missing bars of his signal.

"I think I'd best put you on charge."

He scuttled over to his bag and unzipped it, took out his charger and found a plug socket that was nearest the desk.

"That thing looks medieval!" He mocked the ageing, weary looking socket, "Hopefully it will work. I think the whole place needs rewiring!"

He jammed the charger into an adapter that would allow his American cell phone plug to be used in a British socket, and then put it all in place. The old lights above him fluttered and he seemed to hold his breath for a couple of seconds, silently pleading with it to charge. The battery symbol indicated to him that it was indeed being refuelled.

"Well, at least that's something." Now, he turned his attention to the hallway once again and swallowed hard, the tightness in his chest stabbing away at him.

"For goodness sake, Jack! Get a hold of yourself!" He started to laugh, maybe trying to distract himself from what he had actually seen and what he actually truly felt.

"There is nothing in this house that can hurt you! You're not a kid anymore!"

The wind and rain seemed to attack the house at that point and the lights flickered.

"There is no such thing as ghosts!" He whispered, not daring to raise his voice.

He left the safety of his Grandfathers study and immediately felt the unforgiving cold of the tiled hallway under his bare feet. He rolled his eyes, not quite understanding why he had not put on his socks and shoes again.

Because you've been drunk and unconscious for most of the evening, you idiot! He heard one voice say and smiled. The smile was immediately torn from his face when another much quieter voice hissed another thought.

Because you're scared.

He shook his head in defiance.

"Oh yeah? And what is it I'm supposed to be so scared of?" He said. There was no reply and with an arrogant look now masking his face, he skipped across the cold tiles down the corridor towards the kitchen, which was situated at the rear of the house. He passed the stairs slowly and even with this new false facade of bravery he had created, it still did not instil in him the courage he needed to look up into the darkness that devoured the second floor.

As he made his way to the kitchen he flicked on every light switch that he came into contact with. Light was his saviour, light was hope. There were no bad dreams or shadowy tricks in the light. On some occasions switches failed and he was left to speed up though darker sections of the corridor, letting his hunger drive him forward. He let that be the catalyst that kept him moving and focussing all his attentions on that, not on the sounds upstairs, that thing in his mother's old room, not on the constant rattling of the door knocker in that familiar tune. Not the chiming of the broken clock, the neighing of a horse that he had heard outside and certainly not the dream about the blood pouring from the bathtub's tap. His stomach rumbled again, as if it had some kind of metal detector that sounded off whenever it was getting close to its treasure. He turned a corner and entered what was once known as the servants quarters. In a bygone era, The Heron family had many servants to help with the running of such a large house. Jack's Great Grandfather had staff of around four or five during his reign at the head of the family, a butler, a footman, a cook and maids. Jack remembered his Grandfather saying that his Father lived beyond his means and there was no need for such pretentiousness. When he took the house on he only kept on a maid and a cook. Jack remembered the cook, a plump old lady that had a homely pleasant nature, although he could not remember her name.

"Ms Soaper!" He squealed with excitement, for now he could paint a better picture of her in his head and he seemed to remember more about the lovely old lady. He recalled the ruffles of his hair as she sneaked him cream cakes and not to tell his Mother as it may spoil his dinner. The tweaks of his cheeks when he had run some errands for her, he thought he could have lived without the cheek tugging, but then a part of him felt that he would give anything in the world to feel that again. That warmth, that caring attention, that love.

"Sausage rolls!" He gleamed, "She used to bake the best sausage rolls!"

These pleasant thoughts seemed to spur him forward and he dashed towards the kitchen, ignoring other rooms that seemed to call to him. However he was dazzled by the brightness of such fond memories that these dark rooms could not penetrate his musing and they reached for him to no avail. He felt like a child again running across the tiles, following his nose to the kitchen. He could even smell the delicious aromas of freshly baked bread, the strong smell of lemons (Ms Soaper insisted on cleaning with lemon juice) and those piping hot sausage rolls straight out of the oven. To Jack there was no better smell. He burst into the kitchen and truly expecting to see her egg-shaped frame bent over the oven, giving those sausage rolls a second glazing of milk. His face dropped when he was met by an empty kitchen, that seemed to have gone unloved for so long. Only one place was set at the oak kitchen table now, the remnants of meals past. A placemat with a picture of horses on (of course), a ring stain where a drink would have sat in exactly the same spot every meal, and condiments within arms reach of where he imagined his Grandfather would have eaten his last meals from, alone. His face fell and his body seemed to sag, as if all the exuberance he had just felt had been sucked out of him. He switched on the light and walked across to the refrigerator, he opened it up and was met by rotting vegetables and curdled milk. He sneered at the contents and then his nostrils were attacked by an overpowering smell of mould ridden cheese. Jack could not stand the smell of cheese at the best of times and these were too much for his senses to take. The foul stench weaved its way through his nasal passage and down to the back of his throat. His gag reflex kicked in and he fought it back, before slamming the refrigerator door closed.

"Jesus wept! What a foul..." He stopped to gag and ran to the sink. Luckily for him he did not vomit, he had done enough of that now, surely there was only stomach lining left to leave his gut. He opened up the cupboards, most of them were bare or homing out of date items or the remains of an old mouses nest.

"Even the mice have abandoned this sinking ship." He said when finally he opened up a cupboard that was filled with tin cans.

"Eureka!" He cried, "Baked beans it is then."

CHAPTER 14

Jack had finished his supper, he had been that ravenous by that point that he had eaten the beans cold, and from the tin. He actually found it quite satisfying and it reminded him of his art college days where baked beans, stale bread and last nights cold pizza was the norm. He had not realised that he had been standing by the kitchen window and looking out at the courtyard to the garden for the last twenty minutes or so. He had been that involved in that pleasant musing of his college days and the oh so fond memory of Ms Soaper that he had become shut off from the world. His mind had taken in so much over the last 24 hours that he maybe needed a break. He needed to sink into happy and positive memories before returning to reality. If it even was reality. Jack hoped with all his heart it wasn't, all the things he had already seen and the pain and fear that he had felt. He hoped it was all just a bad dream, a very bad dream. Jack had finally returned to present day and looked out into the courtyard at the rear of Heron House. The storm seemed to have passed over and had left behind it a soft drizzle of rain in its wake. The wind had calmed down and with the storm clouds now gone, the moon had crept out once again as if sensing it was safe to return, and shone like a polished silver coin in the darkness, bathing the courtyard and garden in its soft glow. It looked so peaceful out there to Jack and he breathed a sigh of relief, at that moment he felt like it was indeed a dream and he had finally woken from its haunting clutches. He unlocked the door which led into the garden and opened it up to an ugly serenade from its hinges, like the sound of a virgin violinist playing on untuned strings. He stepped out of the doorway and was met with that unmistakable Welsh air. The fresh moist breeze seemed to chicane through the valleys at breakneck speed before connecting with the exposed flesh on his gaunt face. It forced him back a step out of sheer surprise, but after the initial shock he felt revitalised. It was refreshing as if washing away the manifestations that had been conjured up in his minds eye. He breathed in that air, filling his aching lungs with it, purging them of the tightness that had contorted around them and tortured with its unrelenting grasp. He closed his eyes and let the rain and breeze gently caress his eyelids. He felt wide awake now and opened his eyes to gaze out at what lay in wait for him in the courtyard. The whole area was paved with tired looking paving slabs, that had been neglected and allowed to be consumed with moss. In between some gaps amongst stones, weeds had grown up from underneath with such ferocity that the paving stones themselves had been shifted out of position.

"I guess Grandad didn't have a gardener on hand these past few years." Jack said to himself as he looked out at the courtyard and further a field. The overgrown grass that led up to a hill and the dark outlines of the stables could just about be seen. He squinted to make out the buildings in the distance, and the distant neighing of a horse was carried on the breeze, Jack ignored it and turned his attentions back to the courtyard. The main focal point of the courtyard was the extravagant pond and fountain that the crooked paving stones surrounded. Once this built up stone feature was the envy of all his Grandfather's friends, and he would love to show off this flamboyant piece to anyone that visited the house. He was so very proud of it. The fountain rose high into the sky. A mythical hippocampus painstakingly carved into the stone and water once erupted from its mouth, spraying into the air before cascading down its peculiar contours of its body, and then joining the pond. The pond was exceptionally deep and was where several of his Grandfathers prized koi carp resided at one point. Jack remembered watching them swim around the water lilies, the vibrant oranges and reds of their scales reflected in the cool pool. Jack shuddered when he thought of the water, he had never liked water and couldn't bring himself to go swimming. When he was at college and his friends would frequently visit the swimming baths he would always decline the invitation, making up some excuse or another, never letting on to them that he could not actually swim and feared the water immensely. Those thoughts again snapped him from his haze and instead of visualising the fountain and pond how it used to be, he saw it now for what it was. Its appearance now disheveled and unloved, a layer of moss attached to the weather damaged stone, chipped and worn. The pond still contained water, but it was a sickly dark green colour, and the foliage that had once lived there and taken care of, had been left to become overgrown and now consumed most of the once exquisite piece of craftsmanship.

"Yes, Grandad. You most definitely needed a gardener to look after..." He trailed off as he stood there staring at the fountain, watching as the subtle droplets of rain fell on the surface of the pond water.

"Gardener!" He whispered and had an image of a gardener that once worked for his Grandfather. A stout looking individual, his red face framed by a bushy grey beard, a stern face under the peak of a tweed flat cap.

"Mister..." He thought for a moment, the image now showing a shotgun leant casually over his shoulder. The gardener's manifestation (That Jack had conjured up), was standing right beside the fountain staring at him. No, not staring but glaring eyes of fire, at least that's how it appeared to Jack and he was shaking his head.

"Why can't I think of your name, Mister..."
The gardener shook his head slowly at Jack and his eyes grew wide as he positioned the shotgun in front of him, aiming it straight at Jack. Jack was frozen to the spot and he saw the gardener pull the trigger.
BANG!
The sound erupted in his head and he closed his eyes, convinced that he had just been shot. He opened his eyes slowly and the gardener was gone. He actually checked his torso over for any wounds, but there was nothing.

"Mr Fiddler!" He gasped, "What happened to you, Mr Fiddler?" He seemed to ask himself that question, partly knowing the answer, the answer would not come forth though (like many answers he needed), but he knew that it was not pleasant. Jack stepped out into the drizzle, his feet still bare but unfazed by the damp and cold, he looked up at the night sky, at the moon that as a child he believed was made of cheddar, then his gaze fell on the fountain and the pond again. He had become fixated on the dark substance that filled the pond. It seemed thick and uninviting, but still he continued to stare at it. All the while hundreds of minuscule raindrops fell onto its surface and created small ripples. Each droplet turned silver from the moons glow, like hundreds of falling razor blades slicing through the dark syrupy treacle, unleashing the green tint inside with each insertion. It took him several seconds to register that something black and sphere-like had started to emerge from the pond water. It was a head, thick black hair slicked with moisture dripped down from it onto the surface of the water and then two eyes appeared, yellowy but bright and full of life, standing out from the pale green flesh surrounding it. Whatever this creature was that was beginning to rise out of the pond made eye contact with Jack, and although it's facial features remained submerged, festering flesh rose up underneath those demonic eyes in what appeared to be a sadistic smile. Jack screamed at the top of his lungs and threw himself back into the kitchen, slamming the door and locking it behind him as quickly as possible. He leant up against the door and slid down it, where he sat on the cold tiled floor shaking as though a whole parade of soldiers had just marched over his grave. That fear had taken hold of him again and it sunk its heinous claws into his chest once more.

CHAPTER 15

Jack had finally dragged himself from the cold kitchen floor and scrambled back into the corridor, not daring to look back out onto the courtyard. His heart rate had increased again, and he worried whether it could take much more of these sudden shocks. There were moments today that he thought he was going to go into cardiac arrest. The anxiety viper had slithered in through his ribcage again and choked his soul. That terrifying fiend that had emerged from the pond could not be real. He told himself this again and again, refusing to believe his eyes, or minds eye.

"Stop this, Jack!" He cried, his voice ricocheted down the corridor and escaped into the hallway. That authoritative screech had halted him from what he was about to do, and that was to run. But where too? He did not know, the urge to run away was strong, so very, very strong.

"This is ridiculous!" He told himself shaking his head, as his chest heaved in and out rapidly, "This is the whiskey talking, or all just a nightmare!"

He started to calm down a little and the lights flickered in the corridor, dimming and then bursting back into life. He tried to ignore that and put that down to the house being old, besides he'd already thought that the place probably needed rewiring anyway.

"Lights flicker in old houses." He said firmly, and with that began to make his way back down the corridor that led back to the hallway, or so he thought. He had taken the wrong corridor in his delirium and ended up in the dark part of the house which was known as the servant's quarters. The corridor was in darkness and several doors remained tightly shut on either side of him.

"How did I get down here?" His head felt woozy and the corridor seemed to distort and warp in front of his eyes. He shook off the feeling and when he opened his eyes the corridor looked fresh and vibrant. The carpet, soft under his bare feet and not worn and trodden down like it had been before. Wallpaper was immaculate and everywhere clean and pristine, not like moments ago when he could have sworn that the wallpaper was peeling from the damp walls and cobwebs hung across the ceiling like festive streamers. He heard a voice whisper, "Come on!", it was the voice of a child, a very impatient child, "Come on, come on! You've got to see this!"
Jack's head was on a swivel looking for whoever was talking to him, but he saw nothing or no one.

"Jack! For God sakes come on you dick head!"
He turned back to the corridor in front of him and there was his cousin, Julian.

"Julian?" He murmured.

"You're going to miss it!" Julian whispered again, frantically pulling on Jack's arm to lead him somewhere.
Jack could feel Julian's fingers sinking into his fleshy forearm and found himself crying out "Ow! You're hurting me!" The voice escaped him and it sounded younger, child like.

90

"Stop being a baby! You're always such a dick head! Where is your sense of adventure?" Julian sneered.

Jack suddenly remembered Julian and what an obnoxious little delinquent he was. He was his Auntie Dilys' son and sometimes they came to stay on weekends and school holidays. Julian was two years younger than Jack and Jack thought that he looked around 12 here. Then a dark thought pierced his brain like an icepick.

Julian died when he was 12.

The thought was gone as soon as it came and Jack continued to remember.

14! I would have been 14.

He had had a very sheltered life back then, he imagined playing small children's games like hide and seek with Julian. He once heard his Grandfather say to his Mother that I was being mollycoddled too much and should be allowed to grow up. Julian was always up to mischief and liked to get Jack into trouble. Jack recalled his mother telling him that it was because he didn't have a Father so he had no discipline. It still didn't change the fact that Jack got blamed for most of the things that the precious Julian did.

"Are you coming or not?" Julian asked again, a horrid scowl scaring his temple under a mop of dark hair. Jack did not answer, he was still trying to make sense of it all.

"Suit yourself!" Julian scoffed and headed further down the corridor, towards a bathroom door that stood at the end of the hall. This door was different from all the others, in that it had a frosted glass window in it. It was the servant's bathroom, obviously back then it would not have been the done thing for servants to use their lords and ladies ablutions.

"We'll get caught!" Jack found himself squeaking, again higher in pitch.

Jack noticed that the frosted glass was now lit up and bathed the corridor in a soft ambience. Warm steam seeped from the gap underneath the door and framed it, as the silhouette of a figure from within moved around on the other side of the glass. It all looked so inviting to Jack and he approached it dreamily. Julian was hunched over at the door, his one eye scrunched up, the other pressed against the keyhole.

"You gotta see this, Jack!" Julian salivated and then moved away from the door and beckoned Jack forward enthusiastically. Jack leant forward and his eye met the keyhole, and before him appeared the very sensuous form of Patricia Leon. Jack recalled that Patricia Leon was a maid that was with the Heron Family for a few months while their usual maid, Hattie, was on a leave of absence, due to her brother falling ill. His Grandfather used an agency to fill the position while hattie was predisposed and it was Patricia that was sent to fill the role. Patricia was in her early twenties and French, from a city in the south of France called Toulouse. It was very rare for a small Welsh town to have someone so exotic visiting. Jack believed that she had many a visit from male callers, that his Grandfather would send packing from his door with a tirade of abusive language. Jack could understand why she got so much male attention, she was very beautiful and with her skin of the darker persuasion it added more to her mystique, as Cyfrinach pwynt y De was a predominately caucasian community back then.

"Is that a thing of beauty or what?" Julian's voice muttered in his ear. Jack slowly nodded as he watched Patricia, who was dressed only in a suspender belt and stockings, tiptoe over to the cast iron bath that sat in the middle of the duck egg tiles. She bent over to cut the hot tap off and through the thick warm mist Jack could see the firm ripeness of her buttocks. He heard her sigh and say something in French as she leant over further to retrieve the plug. The bathtub was now almost full to the brim and would obviously overflow when she entered. As she looked for the plug, her cheeks gaped and unveiled her vagina, plump and succulent like ripened fruit. Jack could hardly believe his eyes, nor actually take in what it all meant. There was a strange sensation in the confines of his underpants, something stirred, something almost mythical and unknown to Jack. Water slurped and gulped as it left the bathtub, Patricia remained bent over the tub until she was satisfied she had let out right amount of water. Her rear swayed back and forth as she hummed to herself a pleasant little tune, unbeknownst to her that her every move was being scrutinised by Jack's young green eyes. He was transfixed, what was this primitive stirring and yearning for that protruding bulge of flesh that seemed to called to him. It did not seem real, her light brown buttocks framed in by the suspender belt and stockings, made it look like something on television. She stood up and playfully swivelled on the spot, he could now see all of her, the breathtaking contours of her slender figure, her brown flesh standing out from the white mist that surrounded her. Julian said something, but Jack either could not hear him or chose to ignore him. Maybe Julian was annoyed that he was hogging the keyhole and thought it was his turn to see the delights that lay in wait on the other side of the door. Her breasts were small and pert and in proportion with her long slender frame. His penis started to grow immensely at just the sight of what

93

stood before him and if you'd asked him at that moment why, he would not be able to give you an answer. As her hands worked at tying her dark hair back into a bun, her chest was naturally pushed forward, the dark tips of her nipples being kissed by the moist warm vapour that encased the room. She placed one leg carefully on the side of the bathtub and unclipped the suspenders from her stocking. He noticed that he could see that forbidden fruit again, settled between her legs and a thick mound of black hair spiralled above it. He gaped as her fingertips gently rolled down the stocking, over her knee and down her calf and shin, exposing her toes that were painted an extravagant and garish cerise. Julian had suddenly dragged him away from the keyhole and was groaning at him, but Jack could not hear him as visions of breasts, legs, buttocks and vaginas danced before his mind's eye, as if storing them for future occasions, just in case a moment like this never arises again. Julian looks into the keyhole and then steps away, visually annoyed.

"She's in the bath now! Great, I missed all the good bits!"
This was of course all Jack's fault and he told him so, but Jack was in a daze and his penis was surely going to burst through his underpants and corduroys any second. Jack wanted more, she was like a drug to him and he peered through the keyhole again. He could see her bathing, resting and looking so peaceful and she continued to hum that delightful tune. Julian may be annoyed that he missed what he said were the best bits, but to Jack she was perfection. At peace submerged in the water or standing upright naked.

Was this love? He thought, and then suddenly his romanticising evaporated as Julian pulled down his corduroys and knocked at the glass of the door vigorously before running back up the corridor laughing. Jack could not run due to his trousers shackling him to the spot and he yanked at them quickly to try and get them back up and somehow, make his getaway before Patricia appeared at the door. It was too late. As he gazed up at the open door, warm steam smothered him and Patricia was standing there wrapped in a towel, moisture dripping from her flesh and wearing a very cross expression.

"What are you doing?" She began in a cross tone and then as Jack stood up to try and plead that it was not what it looked like, she noticed the bulge in his underpants that seemed to beg to be let free like some captive wild animal.

"Please..." Jack pleaded, but Patricia cut him off with a shushing sound and then she looked around the corridor, as if to make sure it was empty.

"Come in here now!" She said bluntly.   Jack had always been brought up to do what grown ups had asked him to do and he complied without debate, quickly shuffling into the mist, his trousers still wrapped around his ankles. He stood there wondering what would happen, he didn't know what he had witnessed and what was going on inside his underpants, but he knew what he had done was wrong. Was she going to shout at him or tell his mother? Or smack him perhaps? Ms Soaper would often clip Julian around the ear when he misbehaved in the kitchen, but never Jack, because he very rarely misbehaved. But this was different and he knew it. Patricia shut the door behind her and walked through the moving vapour until she was standing in front of him.

"You think it is okay to peep through keyholes at people, Master Heron?" She asked.

Jack shook his head and looked down at his feet ashamed. As he looked down he could see that unsightly bulge sticking out in front of him and it had started to wane.

"And what is that you are hiding there?" She asked.

"Nothing!" He said.

"You lie! Move your hands." She said.

He did and he stood embarrassed beyond belief.

"This is good no?" She said smiling approaching him.

"What?"

"This how you say..." She tried to think of the English word as she circled him like a vulture does its prey, "Erection! It is good it is pleasurable, no?"

Jack didn't know what to say, and when she yanked down his underpants to join the corduroys he immediately tried to pick them back up.

"Stop." She declared, "Leave them where they are." She was now standing in front of him looking at his penis, which had started deflating rapidly.

"Oh, dear! It would appear that it is leaving us." She sighed, "Let us see if we can do something about this, oui?"

Suddenly she removed her towel and let it fall to the floor, the change in temperature made her nipples hard, Jack's penis joined them and doubled in size immediately.

"Well, that is better, Master Jack!" She smiled and sat on the edge of the bathtub and opened her legs.

"You like this, oui?" She began to rub a slender index finger over the fleshy part of her vagina. His eyes widened and his penis seemed to stretch out further from its sparse nest of red pubic hair. She smiled and stood up again and approached him, she crouched down so that they were at eye level and she caressed the shaft of his penis slowly and gently.

"Do you like that, Master Heron?" She asked softly and before he could answer he ejaculated and grumbled, "Oh God!"

Patricia rose up and laughed at him as he stood with a dripping penis retreating back into its usual comfort zone.

"What am I to do with this limp noodle!" She mocked pointing and laughing.

Tears started to fill in his eyes and he pulled up his garments as quickly as he could and fled hearing her words call to him, "Come back when you are a man, Master Heron!"

Jack stopped running and realised he was in the gloomy corridor of the servants quarters again. He turned back to face the bathroom door that was now in darkness, the frosted window scarred with a fracture across it.

"What in God's name is going on here!" He murmured and then felt the sticky sensation in his underwear, a wet patch appearing through his trousers.

CHAPTER 16

To say that Jack had now sobered up completely was an understatement, he had cleaned himself up and redressed, finding something a bit more casual and comfortable as he sat in his Grandfather's study. Extremely embarrassed, he quickly stuffed the semen stained items into his bag, hiding them from the world, or was it to hide them from himself? He was trying not to think about what had just happened in the servant's bathroom, it felt so real to him, so very real. Her presence, the scent of that cheap French perfume that singed his nostrils and had parched the back of his throat, with its bitter aftertaste. The aroma seemed to linger around inside his head for the longest time. It made him feel dizzy as though he were under the influence of some drug. Even now when brushing his hairy tongue across the roof of his mouth he could still taste it, taste her.

"Bullshit!" He murmured as he continued to put everything back in his bag. He saw her though, he knew that much. Saw the contours of her slim dark body and those slender limbs that seemed to stretch out too far. He stopped as he thought about her naked body that was flaunted before his very eyes. The vapour that rose from the hot bath, he felt it caress his face, leaving behind droplets of moisture on his skin, even the warmth of the water, it was all very real to him.

"It's all just nonsense! Complete and utter nonsense!" Jack scoffed, trying to delude himself, "Past fantasies rearing their heads that's all." He laughed, it was a loud hysterical howl, it could have been mistaken for the neighing of a horse.

"As if that type of thing happens to anyone!" Then his hand stuffed a pair of rolled up socks into his bag and felt the gluey substance that was still clinging to his underpants as an undeniable reminder. It seemed to attach itself to his knuckles as his hand slid into the back and then quickly recoiled in disgust.

Then how do you explain that, Jack? He thought as he examined the stringy gob of semen that had fastened itself to his knuckles and fingers like some undesirable visitor from another planet. His face gurned grotesquely as though he had smelt something untoward and then wiped it away on the fresh laundry that he could see inside the confines of the bag. This event had actually shaken him more than the constant sound of the knocker playing its tune of Rat-a-tat-tat, or the apparition in black that had burst from his Mother's room ordering him to get out. Even more than the shuddering thought of Black Jack, or the gardener with the shotgun or even that creature that peeped out from the pond at him. The reason being he had always felt sexually inadequate, he hadn't had many partners in his life and the times he had tried to have sex he had either failed to become erect or he had been way to premature. Both situations leaving him feeling embarrassed and ashamed. The main reason he did not get romantically involved with anybody anymore, the reason he had never tried to make that step with Marcy.

You'd shoot your load too early, or fail to get the damn thing up! Then that would ruin your relationship and friendship with her and then where would you be? No, it is too damn complicated, she'd probably laugh at you and call you limp noodle anyway.

He'd told himself this many times over and over again, and that may well be the reason why he threw himself into his artwork. It was a way to unleash that pent up sexual frustration he had, and the reason why he could churn out dozens upon dozens of fine pieces of art. He zipped up his bag that now bulged, swollen with clothes that hadn't been folded and homed neatly. He threw it over his shoulder and grabbed his cell phone and charger and made for the hallway. It was very early hours of the morning now and he couldn't stand it any more, he had to get out of this place. But, he stood in the hallway and just looked at the door, the door that he was so terrified to open earlier on. It seemed just as terrifying to open it to leave.

Rat-a-tat-tat still played for him as he stood frozen to the spot. He hadn't wanted to think about it but the wind had stopped over an hour ago yet that rising stallion in black cast iron kept on rapping at the door.

What if there is somebody on the other side of that door?

He swallowed hard and gooseflesh again covered his skin, Jack was absolutely terrified of this house and the shadows of the past that seemed to manifest themselves at every chance they got.

"I need to leave!" He murmured.

Rat-a-tat-tat! Came the reply from the house.

"I said I need to leave!" He groaned, tears swelling in his eyelids.

Rat-a-tat-tat! It grew louder.

"Let me out!" He barked, crying freely now as the knocker unleashed an unrelenting tirade on the door, it was deafening and vicious.

"LET ME FUCKING OUT OF HERE!" He screamed at the top of his lungs and then there was silence. Jack breathed heavily and that was the only sound in the hallway. If the Grandfather clock had been working there would have been ticking to keep him company, but at this moment in time, all he heard was the steady staggering hiccup of breathes.

He looked around and was about to take that Herculean task of reaching for the doorknob when the door knocker broke into life again.

RAT...A-TAT...TAT. It announced ever so slowly, the pause between each strike was horrifying, as though there was indeed someone orchestrating its rhythm. Jack with eyes like saucers, trembled and clutched his phone, instinctively glancing at the screen to see if he could indeed make an emergency call. But who would he call? What would he say? The no signal sign saved his blushes of any such conversation with emergency services.

RAT-A-TAT-TAT!RAT-A-TAT-TAT!RAT-A-TAT-TAT!RAT-A-TAT-TAT!RAT-A-TAT-TAT!RAT-A-TAT-TAT! RAT-A-TAT-TAT!RAT-A-TAT-TAT!

It came in an overwhelming barrage and Jack fled, but only up the stairs, tripping once and making the mistake of turning around for a last glance at the door. A small frosted window at the side of the door seemed to have a shape behind it, the shape of a figure, and it was moving! A face peering into the frosted glass to try and catch a sneak peek into the hallway. Eyes widening again he escaped to the landing and the darkness.

GET OUT! Cascaded over him in a chilling breeze.

There was seemingly no immunity or safe place within these walls as he stumbled and ran down the dark corridor.

GET OUT! GET OUT! GET OUT! GET OUT! GET OUT! GET OUT! GET OUT! GET OUT! GET OUT!

The words pursing him in his escape.

Escape? Where to?

He burst through a bedroom door and dove under the covers of a small bed, where he remained for the rest of the night, drifting in and out of sleep to the depressing harmonies that the Heron House band perform tirelessly.

CHAPTER 17

Jack must have been around 8 years old when he crept across the landing towards his Father's room. He kept his latest piece of artwork rolled up and hidden in his back pocket of his jeans. He had to keep it hidden from his Mother, since his Father had become severely ill, she had taken to drinking very heavily and unfortunately for Jack she would take it out on him. She didn't like Jack going in his Father's room, especially when he needed to rest.

"Your Father needs to rest, Jack!" She had said to him on many occasion, "He doesn't need you pestering him with your silly drawings now does he?"

Things like this had hurt Jack immensely, sometimes she had even gone so far as to snatch his drawings and rip them up or throw them on the fire. Jack had often watched his hard work get chewed up and spat out into tiny glowing sparks, as the orange flames reflected in his rolling tears. In her own way she probably believed what she was doing was for the best, trying to shield her son from the horrors of the world. The cancer that had taken her husband and started to eat a little piece of him away each day was not for the eyes of small children. She must have believed that seeing his Father degenerate in such a way would have a negative lasting effect on him, but in fact keeping him away from his dying Father only made things worse in the long run. He scuttled down towards his Father's room, and put his ear to the door. He could hear him breathing, it was heavy and uneven, then it would stop all together for what seemed like the longest time and as Jack held his breath too, mimicking his severely ill Father, not out of jest but of fear, hoping that it wasn't his last. A cough and a splutter would erupt and then the stammered breathing would continue again. Jack breathed a sigh of relief and then tried the doorknob, knowing that his Father was now probably awake. The door knob turned and luckily the door opened. His mother had taken to locking the door but sometimes in her drunken haze, she would forget. He paused at the door for a moment, his hand clasped around the bronze doorknob, door hanging ajar. He took a second to check the coast was clear, praying that his Mother was not around to foil his visit. He had shuffled inside, taking his art piece out of his back pocket and unrolling it. Slowly and quietly he made his way to the bed. The room smelt medicinal to him, like a hospital, but also very musty, with the stale scent of flatulence and sweat in the air. His Mother refused to open the window incase he got a chill and made him worse, when the fresh Welsh air may have done him the world of good. The room was gloomy. The curtains always closed and as light sliced through a gap in the curtain, Jack watched as particles of dust floated across the beam. If he was asleep he would leave his creations on the bedside table and hope he would get to see them, before his Mother would undoubtedly remove them. Jack never knew what happened to the drawings that he managed to give his Father, again surmising that they were retrieved by his Mother and destroyed. He approached the bed and his Father stirred, he was frail and gaunt, his cheekbones protruding out further than Jack remembered. His eyes seemed to have sunken into the deep sockets of his skull and his skin seemed to have been caressed with a thin layer of varnish.

"Well, hello there, little man." His Father said and smiled. It seemed to take an abundance of effort to even do something that was so trivial, "Have you got something for me?"

Jack nodded and smiled back as he handed him the art piece he had drawn. This particular one was of a horse, beautifully constructed and shaded with various yellow tones. Jack had been practicing his colouring and had realised that the harder he pressed down with the pencil crayon the darker the colour appeared, this helped him to create several different tones.

"It's a yellow horse." His Father smiled again, the pain was plain to seen in his faded marbled eyes, "It must be Honeybutt! Am I right?"

Jack nodded back beaming with enthusiasm.

His Father put out his hand and Jack held it in his, it weighed nothing, the skin almost transparent over skeletal digits.

"Jack..." But, that was all he managed before his mother burst into the room in a whirlwind of angst, shrieking at him to get out! His Mother tugged at the scruff of his neck to throw him out of the room and as he looked back at his Father for help, the skin started to rot and peel away from his face, leaving behind a jittering skull.

Jack screamed and woke up in a puddle of his own sweat.

"Dad!" He yelled to no one, maybe to his spirit, or to the house itself. If there were such things as ghosts, and that was indeed what he had been witnessing, then why could he not see his Father? He longed to see his Father, converse with him, cuddle him (when his Father was strong enough too), kiss him and just love him. He very rarely got the chance and before he knew it his Father had passed on. He longed to have that time back and would have given anything, or everything to have a moment with him again. The dream he remembered was like a rerun of some classic episode of his life, he remembered it all (apart from the final nightmare that he turned into) it was a real event that happened, as real as life gets because that was the last time he got to see his Father. He died the next day.

"Oh, Dad!" He wept. "Oh, how I miss you."

He lay back down and although it was daylight outside he drifted back to sleep, the question lingering, "What were you going to say to me, Dad? What were your last words going to be to me?"

As he cried himself to sleep, he realised that it was a question that he would never have an answer to.

CHAPTER 18

Jack finally woke up. A thick haze had descended upon him as his eyelids struggled to peel themselves open, tearing away the gluey layer of mucus that had built-up around his exhausted eyes. His head was swimming in a cocktail of bad dreams, disorientation and the repercussions of too much Scotch. He slowly sat up, his movements were sluggish as if he were being wound up by a mechanical key, only being allowed to rise upright each time the key was turned. Finally he reached a seated position and groaned. He resembled an ancient vampire that you may see in an old British horror film, rising from the confines of its coffin after a days rest.

"Oh God, my head!" He moaned and grabbed at his temples, "Where the bloody hell am I anyway?" He added looking around at a small room, smothered in cobwebs.

In his drowsy gaze he took in his surroundings and then the penny dropped and he realised he was in his childhood room.

"Well, I'll be damned!" He said smiling, his face and cheeks actually ached from the strain of such an effort as his face felt like those specific muscles had not been used in a while, certainly while he had been here in Heron House anyway. The memories of time spent playing in his childhood bedroom were pleasant. Nostalgia swept over him as he visualised those Saturday afternoons as the sun burst through the window and he played with his toys on the carpet, situated in the warm patch and feeling content. Or those evenings spent under the covers with his torch reading comics or drawing his favourite super heroes. His soul was delighted to receive something positive to mull over. The bedroom was in fact a place of solitude for a young Jack, he could escape there and could forget all the worries and confusions that were occurring behind his door. His Mother would not shout at him or put him down while he was in his room, she didn't bother about him when he was out of sight and that suited him just fine. She couldn't tell him his drawings were a waste of time and he'd never get anywhere in life doing such childish things. He never understood how something could be a waste of time if you enjoyed doing it. If it made you happy then how could it ever be a waste of time? This was how a young Jack's mind worked and he was indeed right on all accounts. Jack loved his mother but he used to feel guilty about thoughts he had about her. He would think that he prefer his old Mother, the one that was around before his Father became ill. It actually felt to Jack when he was younger that he had had two Mothers, because the change was so bizarre, he often compared his Mother (or indeed Mothers) to Dr Jekyll and Mr Hyde. Yes, his bedroom was a safe space and the poisons of the world could never filter in here. When he was there his Father wasn't dying, his Mother wasn't an alcoholic, he didn't have to play with Julian and he was away from the horses.

"Horses." He whispered and all at once remembered where he was. He blinked away the blurred vision of yesteryear and focused on the dark lifeless box that was once that place of protection. The horses reference seems to plague him, he felt so utterly afraid of horses, but he could not remember why. His fond memories spent with his Grandfather talking about horses and riding them with his Grandfather's supervision, were all incredibly pleasing. He would draw and paint pictures of horses all the time, and even had a jockey outfit when he was only a toddler.

"Horses... When did this sense of dread about horses take hold of me? I mean I still paint them today! Most of my famous work that I have produced has featured a horse in it." He puzzled not understanding when this could have happened. He manoeuvred himself onto the edge of the very small bed and stood up, his joints serenading him with the anthem of an uncomfortable nights sleep. He looked around again at the room, it had none of his toys or books, or anything that would disclose that he ever lived here, all that remained was old dusty furniture.

"Horses?" He murmured again, trying to make some sense of it all, he had woken up with a fresh open mind, not really remembering what had happened yesterday, but it was as though he had gone into some kind of detective mode and had a need to find answers. He slunk over to the window, picking up his cell phone from the floor, it must have spilled out of bed in the night. The battery showed 32% and he looked on bemused.

"How long have I been asleep?" He then glared at the time that stared back at him in large white font which announced to him that it was nearly four o'clock in the afternoon.

"The day's nearly gone! Must have been a rough night!" He said placing the phone on the windowsill. Suddenly he was hit by a piercing headache, like he had had before he arrived at the house, the memories exploding in his head all at once and he dropped to the floor, fingers gripping tugging at his hair. That thing in his

109

Mother's room hissed at him to, 'GET OUT!'. The naked maid laughing at his useless flaccid penis, his Father as some kind of rotting zombie, the creature dwelling in the pond, Mr fiddler unleashing the contents of his shotgun at him, the bathtub filled with blood.

"Oh, God, Oh Jesus Christ! What is wrong with me? Can't somebody help me?" Rat-a-tat-tat could be faintly heard in the distance, downstairs in the hall the sound of the constant knocking spiralled and clambered up the staircase and was behind his door.

"I must get out of here! I don't care anymore about the deeds to this Godforsaken house! It can rot to its foundations for all I care!" He screamed and tears streamed down his face.

Jack pulled himself up using the windowsill, his legs jittering on the spot as though he was doing some vintage dance from the sixties. He grabbed for his cell phone, there was still no signal, no help, no hope.

Rat-at-tat-tat! Rat-at-tat-tat! Rat-at-tat-tat! The sound came louder again and seemed closer. Was it at his door?He stared at the photo again of himself with Marcy and the tears came again.

"Marcy I swear if I get out of this I'm going to tell you how much I love you and how much you mean to me, damn it!"   T h e knocking stopped. Jack sniffed up the mucus that ran from his nostrils and wiped at his eyes, he looked around and thought that it was very odd that it had just abruptly ended like that.

His eyes grew wide again as an answer to an earlier question had finally been resolved. He turned to look out the window and could see the dark buildings in the hills of the Heron estate, the stables rising out of the gloomy landscape, misshapen and eery like a silent graveyard.

"Black Jack!" He whispered.

CHAPTER 19

After forcing himself to get dressed and have some breakfast/ lunch, which happened to be another tin of baked beans, Jack ventured out of the house. Although he'd only spent one full day with the confines of Heron house, to him it had felt like at least a month. He felt cut off from the world and civilisation, which sometimes isn't a bad thing, but when you're pretty spooked from what you believe to be a haunted house, being alone is the last thing you need. The front door had still been relentlessly rattling out its little tune and still Jack could not bring himself to use that door, for the fear inside him still told him that if he did indeed open that door, he would not like what lay in wait. He had taken the back door out onto the garden patio, passed the fountain and pond. He tried with all his will not to acknowledge the ponds existence and climbed over a decrepit fence that led to a neighbouring field. It was still Heron land, but sections of the land had been split up by wooden fences so that the horses had room to roam when needed. Times had definitely changed now, the fences were once all uniform and precise, now most of the beams lay next to the slanting posts, splintered and disheveled by years of abuse from that stiff Welsh weather and nobody seemed to care about its wellbeing anymore. Jack had discovered just how harsh the Welsh weather could be long ago, but again his memory seemed to shut out such information. He had awkwardly scaled the fence, the sodden wooden structure causing him to slip several times.

"These designer shoes are definitely not made for orienteering!" He scoffed as he came down on the other side in an uncomfortable thick carpet of mud that was concealed under the grass that was overgrown and nearly up to his knees.

"Oh great!" He groaned, lifting his feet out of the mire with an unpleasant squelching noise.

He sighed and shook his head.

"Nope, they are most definitely not made for such exploits."

He trudged through the mud and overgrowth and on a few occasions what Jack believed to be some kind of animal pat, which was not at all pleasing to his nostrils when it had been disturbed. He stopped at the top of a hill and felt the wind devour his face. He closed his eyes and allowed it to attack him, it was a very satisfying experience and it seemed to wash away the cobwebs that were tangled with bad memories. He felt cleansed by it and he even did a little spin on the spot with his arms held out either side.

"Whoop!" He shouted at the top of his voice, "I feel like Julie Andrews!" He laughed, but suddenly became dizzy and fell down into the moist shards of grass. He chuckled to himself and lay back in the damp meadow, looking up at those dark clouds that seemed to be rapidly devouring the afternoon sky. He sat up and gripped his knees, looking out at the distance, the fields, the hills, valleys it really is a beautiful sight. He watched as those clouds seemed to increase in speed, crashing into each other like unrelenting dodgems at some travelling gypsy fair.

"No doubt those bastards will be bringing more rain with them." Jack said and climbed to his feet, brushing off the dirt from his trousers, smiling and thinking to himself what was the point. He looked back at the house and that shudder rattled his spine again, as if it were being played like a xylophone. He realised the reason he felt happy again was because he was away from that place. Even from here he could see the windows that appeared to watch his every move, not allowing him too far out of their sight, he wondered whether there were any of those apparitions spying on him. That thought made him shudder again and he could still faintly hear the Rat-a-tat-tat riding on the breeze. He pictured the red of the front door wagging like a tongue calling him back home. He felt sick again and the taste of baked beans endeavoured to make a second appearance, but he fought the urge and turned around to look at the field that lay in front of him and not too far in the distance stood the stables.

He stood in the field motionless as the breeze attacked him, his clothes fluttered erratically against his body. His hair rose into the air and flopped around like a flag on a mast. He was literally scared stiff by what lay before him. Steadfast in the middle of an overgrown field he resembled a living, breathing scarecrow, and with the gaping look of horror that was etched on his face, no crow or other winged pest would dare torment him.

He brushed his flailing mop of hair away from his face, but it returned immediately, annoyingly swatting him in his face.

"The stables…" He started and then trailed off to silence. The dark wooden structures were broken and fractured, splintered beams burst out of burnt out frames, the sad remains of what would

114

have once been stables. A fire that had taken place had charred half of the buildings, turning the remnants black and brittle. Burnt wood spat out in all directions like the jagged horns of some prehistoric beast. The other side of the stables remained intact and unburnt, but still just as menacing, as shadows appeared to cut through the doorways and make them look like slanting, distrustful eyes. He hadn't set out to visit the stables when he left the house, far from it, it was probably the last place he wanted to be at this moment in time. Something seemed to have pulled him here, something in his subconscious had manipulated him and brought him here. The wind swirled around him whispering in his ears, with it the wind brought sounds, the banging of a door knocker, the hissing of some harpy telling him to 'Get out!', the neighing of a horse.

"Black Jack!" He murmured again.

He could no longer fight the inevitable and threw up. It burnt his throat and then lay at his feet the colour of tangerine peel, peppered with several rounded lumps.

"I can't do this! I can't go in there it's been too long!" Flashes of the past suddenly entered his mind and violently lashed dark deeds in front of his minds eyes.

"I can't!" He wailed and suddenly the breeze seemed to cease. He suddenly saw Julian, again as a twelve year old boy, in the distance by the entrance to the stables. He gestured to him, waving him over to follow him before disappearing into the stables courtyard.

"Curiosity killed the cat, Jack." He told himself, or was it more like a warning, either way unfortunately Jack was already walking towards the old stables.

CHAPTER 20

Jack's designer shoes that were now smothered in a heavy layer of mud touched down on the gravelled surface of the stable courtyard. The sound of small stones being forced to disperse under his sole was carried for miles on the dancing breeze. He stopped and looked around at the misshapen wooden structures, they seemed sad and lonely, forgotten by a world that once loved them. They had been used to home creatures of power and pride, they had been used to people coming and going on a daily basis, fixing them up if there was ever a problem or giving them a fresh lick of paint if they were looking a tad sorry for themselves. Those days had long gone. Jack looked around and took it all in.

"Doesn't look like this place as seen any TLC for a few years." That made him feel almost mournful as though the broken ruins were the headstones of loved ones. The smell of burnt wood still lingered around, being swept up his nostrils by that breeze, a breeze that seemed to be growing wilder. A warning perhaps that another storm was well on its way. The wind circled him, cocooning him in a brisk shroud and as it whistled around and around him, he heard what he thought was the neigh of a horse. The wind dispersed and he looked on at the stables and its courtyard. It had somehow sprung to life, appearing to him how it did all those years ago. People rushed around taking care of their daily duties. Looking after the horses was a full time job and Jack's Grandfather employed the best people for the job. He gazed around in awe feeling like a child again. He saw the majority of the horses he knew from growing up, all those that were hung in the study, on prestigious 'Wall of Champions' to be remembered forever.

"Blue Bottle!" He cried, his voice a high pitch screech, like that of a child. The grey horse trotted in front of him, being led by the reins, in the glimmering sun of yesteryear he almost appeared metallic, like some futuristic robot horse.

"Red Admiral!" He squealed again, trotting forward to stroke him as the stable lad brushed her long dark mane.

"Hello, Jack!" The stable boy spoke and looked at him with a mischievous smile, "I've gotta clean Red Admiral's sheath. Wanna help?"

Jack's stomach turned and the stable boy burst into hysterics. Cleaning the smegma that had built up on a horse's penis was really not Jack's idea of fun.

"Dirty job, but someone's got to do it, Jack!"

"Well, it isn't going to be me!" He heard his voice reply, distant and quiet.

"Run along then." The stable lad chuckled as he led Red Admiral away to a stable, that just minutes ago had lay burnt and barren.

"Oh, that bloody Julian is around here somewhere." The stable lad echoed, "If he plays the horses up again, tell him I'll tan his arse for him!" Jack looked around again, he saw Julian hiding behind a barrel that was filled to the brim with water. He gestured to

Jack again, he looked mischievous like some little goblin or mythical woodland creature.

"What are you doing, Julian?" He whispered and started to walk towards him. He walked straight into Mr Fiddler, the gardener who was forking hay into an empty stable.

"Careful now, Jack!" He grumbled, leaning on his pitchfork, as the sun kissed his bald head that glistened with sweat. He thought he heard himself apologise and Mr Fiddler smiled at him.

"Don't let that little shit get you in trouble, Jack. Be a Shepard not a sheep, lad." He turned around and carried on with his duties. He could feel his cheeks ripen as if he were smiling from ear to ear. He liked Mr Fiddler, he always used to look out for him and sneak him chocolate bars, but Mr Fiddler hated Julian. He looked around at all the different horses being groomed or rode, all their different coloured coats shimmering in the afternoon sun, and just seeing the place so full of life gave him that sweet nostalgic feeling in the pit of his stomach again. The gruff neighing of the horses did not scare him, like that sound in his dream from that black stallion. The smells of straw and even the potent aroma of horse manure was not unpleasant for it felt real, like the good times of the past, good times that he struggled to remember.

"How could I ever be scared of this place? It's magical!" He said, his voice sounding closer this time and more grown up. He watched as Julian disappeared into one of the stables near the end of the one row. As children they were forbidden to enter the stables alone, Jack knew this and knew that Julian was up to no good but... "Curiosity killed the cat, Jack!" And with those words in his head he crept across the courtyard to the stable.

118

As he approached the stable, everything seemed to appear gloomy, like a dark cloud had descended and hung over him and the stable like a hungry vulture. Everyone had disappeared and there came a ruckus from the stable he was now walking cautiously towards. It was as if he had been lassoed around the waist and now he were being slowly pulled towards it, against his will. The ruckus sounded like what he had heard in his Mother's room at the house last night but surely it couldn't be? He cringed in horror that he would enter that stable and that dark harpy, with its large gaping maw would be lying in wait. She would not have to tell him to 'Get out' this time, he would surely do that of his own accord. The Dutch doors swung gently to and fro against the breeze, in no real pattern. They did not move in unison, but what did cry in unison was the hinges, grating away with every movement almost like a warning. Jack was powerless to heed such a warning and reaching the doors, slunk in between them and entered the stable. Pitch black greeted him and whatever uproar that had been taking place before he entered had now ceased. All there was for him was darkness and nothing else.

"Hello? Julian, where are you?" He meekly squeaked.

He heard the giggling of a child and span around in time to see the doors slammed shut behind him.

"No!" He gasped.

The bolts were suddenly viciously slammed into the locks.

"No!" He yelled, "Help!"

His cries for help were a mixture of old and new. The young high pitched shriek sounded familiar and terrifying, the sort of gut wrenching sound a parent would never want to hear coming from their own child. The other cry was close, very close, it came from him and it was very, very real. He tried the doors in vain, tugging at them with all his might but these doors were meant to keep huge powerful stallions in, there was no way he could budge them. He heard Julian giggle on the other side of the doors, he could see him spying on him through splits in the wood.

"Julian! This isn't funny, now let me out of here!"
Julian's eyes gleamed, looking almost as yellow as tree sap, as he laughed again and then disappeared. Jack could hear the pitter patter of his feet on the stoney courtyard as he ran away.

"Julian!" He called, to no avail.
Swaddled in silence and darkness, Jack heard something, it sounded like something breathing, heavily.

"Is someone there?" He asked nervously, hoping and praying that it would not be that apparition again.
The breathing did not belong to a human being, the pattern was different. Each breath was strong and almost vicious in its repetition, as if it had lungs the size of beachballs, expanding to their maximum and then relaxing bringing with it a wave of sickeningly hot air. Jack's eyes started to adjust to the dim. Shards of sunlight sliced through the cracks in the stable wall, there was something in the corner, something huge!

"Who is that?" Jack asked, his voice warbling, its tone like that of a frightened child.
He was met by a grunting snort, and then that warm air filled the darkness. He could see the warmth of its breath drift past the shards of sunlight in front of him but still could not work out what was lurking in that dark corner. He felt drawn into the darkness. There was no way of stopping his approach, even though in his head he

120

was screaming to halt and just hightail it out of there. It was no good, there was no stopping his stride, it was almost as though he had lived this before and it was playing out in front of him, knowing how it ended but still no way to stop it from happening. This was a feeling that he had felt several times since arriving, like everything he is seeing has already happened but still he had no memory of any of it. The sound of straw crunching and shuffling across the coarse wooden floor is now all that could be heard on the outside but on the inside Jack's heart was beating at such a rapid succession that it filled his ears. He stopped, sensing that he was near to something. He could smell the sweat radiating off whatever it was causing a hot shroud of vapour around it. The heavy breathing had returned, only it was quicker now, wilder and angry. It moved. Whatever it was, was huge and just an anxious twitch from it shook the wooden structure in its wake. Heavy feet fell on the wooden flooring in quick succession, with a sound like mallets striking chisels. Those aggressive stomps from its hooves reminding Jack of a children's story he used to read.

"Please don't eat me Mr Troll, for I am just skin and bones!" He whispers to himself.

A neighing roar is enough to draw Jack back out of his fairytale musing and back to stare the reaper in its face again. Jack became frozen to the spot and as it moved past, one of the stripes of light cut through the close air and he saw an eye, a dark round eye as large as an apple, shining almost red with a dark crimson undertone to it, full of menace and hate.

"Oh, no!" Jack whimpered under his breath as it moved again and snorted through flaring nostrils. He felt the moist heat on his face as it stepped out of the corner and its dark confines.

"Black Jack!" He cried.

The gigantic black stallion bounded out of the corner, his hooves the size of a medieval knight's mace pounding the wooden flooring furiously. Each attack like a fork of lightning, causing the floorboards underneath them to tremor, Jack almost loosing his footing under the splintering wave. Black Jack shook his head violently, as he strode from side to side his thick black tail caused a breeze against frightened Jack's face like the cracking of a lion tamer's whip. He stared into those ferocious looking eyes, now appearing bright red like the rear lights of a car, that glares at him from up ahead on some dark, lonely highway. In that moment he was consumed with fear but in a split second of clarity he turned to run for the door. He reached the door but it was obviously still locked and there was no way of escape. He banged on it with balled up fists, screaming and hollering to be let out. He daren't turn around, he could hear the audacious stomping and neighing of Black Jack behind him, both sounds getting louder and louder, he knew that he was drawing closer. On the other side of the stable he could faintly hear the voices of Mr Fiddler, the stable lad and even his Grandfather, the calls so faint, so far away. Suddenly there was silence. Had the beast become subdued by something? Jack turned and realised that was not the case. Black Jack towered over him, breathing hot mucus all over him and then it rose. To Jack it seemed to happen in slow motion, he could see this gargantuan black beast rising before him, filling the stable like some mythical kraken from

122

the sea, shadows seeming to flare out from it like waves. Jack collapsed into a frightened heap on the floor, the wood panels still moving underneath him as he sat helpless. Black Jack reared, nostrils flaring and hot air erupting from them as though they were geysers. It's boulder like hooves sparred in the air like a boxer fighting his own shadow and as Jack yelped one more time Black Jack brought everything down onto of him. For a while there was nothing and Jack could feel his chest struggling to recover his normal breathing pattern, his lungs felt crushed under fragments of fractured ribs. A light suddenly filled the darkness as the stable door was opened, there was a figure standing there and it ran to his aid.

"Grandad..." He rasped and then his eyes shut again to darkness.

Jack sat up in a clammy sweat, gasping for air. He looked around to see himself still in the stable but it was now dilapidated, with half the roof missing. No longer did its corners home such terrifying beasts. The stable door swung open and closed, unrelentingly following the flow of the wind.

"Black Jack! You bastard! Now I remember..." He panted.

He had now realised why he had such a fear of horses, it may have appeared to him like an apparition, like a ghost but he could remember this actually happening, this was a memory.

He gasped again for air, holding his ribcage in his shaking hands.

"At least I'm still intact."

Rain had started to fall again, those rapidly approaching cluster of clouds had finally caught up with him and the heavens began to open. As the storm grew the stable doors sang, Rat-a-tat-tat as they harmonised with the blusterous Welsh wind.

CHAPTER 21

Jack had sauntered back down the hill and towards the house in somewhat of a trance, Black Jack's attack feeling so real to him that his chest still felt like it had been fractured into a million pieces. He hadn't really noticed the rain until he had reached the courtyard and sat down on the fountain to try and put together all the jigsaw pieces that seemed to be scattered around inside his head.

"But, it can't be real..." He trailed off for a moment shaking his head, torrential rain lashing down on him, which he totally ignored.

"None of it! Can it?"

As he sat he could hear the rain falling, pitter-pattering on the surface of the pond. The sound was almost hypnotic and seemed to suddenly slow down to his ears. Each drop that kissed the water sounding like a stone being thrown into it, slicing through the surface and causing ripples on the surface of the dark green pond like some psychedelic kaleidoscope. Small bubbles started to develop on the surface, expanding before bursting into moss green flashes. Jack's attention was aroused by this and half in a daze turned around while still sitting on the edge of the fountain and faced the mass of bubbles, all erupting in one spot. He gazed at the centrepiece of the pond, that once beautiful hippocampus, now standing worn, tired and covered in some kind of moist green fungus.

"I used to hold you didn't I?" He asked while looking at the gargantuan stone structure. The bubbles are now larger on the surface of the water, raindrops spearing them before they can burst on their own accord.

"Yes, I did!" He smiled and stood up, "Hide and seek." He murmured and strangely found himself standing in the pond, water up to his knees and overgrown foliage tugging at his thighs as he waded through towards the centrepiece, that had once been his Grandfather's pride and joy. The bubbling stopped as Jack neared the stone creature, he caressed its rough, moist surface with his fingertips. All the while the rain fell and the bubbles returned behind him, larger, and now bursting in rapid succession.

"Yes, it was hide and seek wasn't it? I think I remember now!" He smiled, rain pouring down his face as he climbed onto the small stone base where the hippocampus rose up from to form the actual fountain. His feet slid on the wet surface and he groped for something to cling onto, he grasped the stone structure and managed to keep himself out of the water. He hugged it tightly and all of a sudden he remembered being a child hiding there and hearing Julian shouting, "No fair!"
He laughed to himself, "Tag! It was tag that we played!"
The bubbles rumbled away angrily on the ponds surface, forming quickly as though the water were being boiled.

"Yes! Julian could never get me here because he couldn't swim and hated the water." He laughed and howled like some crazy man, and a crazy man he would appear to anyone seeing him crouching down and clutching a fountain in the middle of a pond, while a rainstorm carried on around him. Something stirred in the water, a black dome shape cut through the surface and seemed to watch Jack.

"Water?" Jack said to himself, wearing a cautious look on his face, "But, it's me that doesn't like water, I can't swim... scared... of..." A drenched figure rose from the pond, skin almost green and caked with all manner of algae, it was skeletal and naked, small in stature and its flesh looked rotten.

"...water!" Jack whispered and turned to see this demonic water goblin standing before him. Its eyes burned yellow, out of dark sunken sockets, and jet black hair clung to its face, completely drenched.

"J-Julian?" Jack trembled, his feet sliding on the moist stone and he was clinging on for dear life now. The thing grinned and as it opened its mouth, a thick black substance proceeded to spew from it, staining its pointed teeth green.

"No!" Jack wailed but it was too late, the demon was on him and with sharp pinching clutches it had seized him, and pulled him into the pond. Jack gasped for air and splashed around in water that now felt like it was bottomless. Without the bottom of the pond to touch or safely tread on, Jack panicked and splashed around in a frenzied outburst. Finally he calmed and floated for a moment, he composed himself but still could not feel the bottom of the pond, he had focussed on the house.

"Okay, just focus, Jack. Let's just get it together and get back to the..."

There was a tug on his leg and he was submerged under water, again panic struck and struck hard as his leg was being tugged again and again, it was almost playful. Then he was grabbed around the throat

126

and dragged down deep. Fighting for his life, he flailed in the water with this dark demonic water goblin, which was now gripping him around the throat and Jack's eyes grew wide as he came face to face with the corpse of his cousin Julian. The yellow eyes glowing under the water as though they were two torches being shone directly at him, that is just how bright they appeared to Jack in the dark waters. Then Julian smiled again, teeth as sharp and needle like as a piranhas! Black gunk oozing from his wild gaping smile. Jack thought that he meant to kill him or eat him, or maybe even both! Suddenly there was a loud gunshot, that erupted above them, causing the water to ripple rapidly and their deathly underwater dance was over, Julian disappeared into the depths of the undergrowth of the pond. Jack burst from the pond, and latched on to the small stone wall that surrounded the pond, he thought that he may never let go of it as he struggled to fill his lungs with air. He looked around but he saw no one, and wondered what could have made that noise. He stayed there for a few moments until he felt a tug on his ankle again, with a scream he flung himself out of the pond and onto the courtyard, panting hard.

"Oh, good God! I don't think I can take much more of this!" He lay looking up at the darkened sky that swept flurry after flurry of rain down on him, he was about to breathe a sigh of relief when that grotesque figure of Mr Fiddler appeared looming over him, loading cartridges slowly into his shotgun. Jack screamed again as he saw Mr Fiddler standing over him, half his face and throat blown away, flesh flapping in the cold air and one good eye glaring at him. Jack scrambled to his feet and headed for the back door that lead into the kitchen but it was locked and no matter how much he tugged at the

127

doorknob it was never going to open. Mr Fiddler, snapped the gun into place and strolled towards him, lifting the gun to aim at him.

"This is all your fault!" Mr Fiddler rasped, Jack could see his tongue wagging and his jaw saying the words through the huge hole in his face. He fired a shot at Jack and it whistled past him and exploded on the wall of the house. Jack screamed and ran around the side of the house when he heard Mr Fiddler growl, "ALL YOUR FAULT, JACK!".

He didn't look back as he raced around the corner of the house and he heard the gun erupt again. Brick explodes behind him, showering him as he made his escape towards the front of the house. He fell over onto the gravel, scrambling and crawling, he then managed to find his feet and was up and running again for the front door. He finally cared nothing for that Rat-a-tat-tat and burst into the hallway, rain and wind came with him as it attacked the inside of the house. He stood panting and completely drenched but there was complete silence in the house. He waited, he could feel something in the pit of his stomach, that something was about to happen. The clock struck and chimed, he turned to face the it. The clock still showed no signs of working but it chimed again and again, six times in total. Then it stopped and there was silence once again, until he heard a shriek that seemed to rise up out of nowhere. It hurtles across the landing and down the stairs. Towards him swooped the dark apparition with the gaping hole in its face, sucking and slurping as it wailed "GET OUT!". He scrambled backwards, falling through the doorway and the door slammed shut. The stallion knocker was flicking back and forth against the door again, in that now ever so familiar Rat-a-tat-tat. Jack got to his feet and ran away from Heron House, with no intention of ever coming back.

CHAPTER 22

Jack collapsed into a heap on the wet cobbles that shined with moisture, as if each one had been treated with a thin layer of varnish. He exhaled heavily, trying with all his might to catch his staggering breaths, stitch pain stabbing at his internal organs like narrow daggers. The rain continued to assault him from every angle and had done so on his entire journey from the house to the town. A journey born out of panic, that started as a sprint, then slowed into a jog and ended in a shuffle, before wilting like a dying flower. Through the blurred vision of exhaustion he glanced up and saw The Old Cock Inn, standing in front of him. He didn't know why he came here, the people inside were not very hospitable the first time around but it was the only place he could think of going. There were people there, safety in numbers, no ghastly spirits could haunt him now. In the back of his mind he remembered the old woman.

"Crowfoot... Mrs Crowfoot!" He gasped.

He saw the pub door swing open and the light from inside beamed out and attacked his sensitive eyes, shadows danced across the beam of light and Jack looked down at a puddle below him. The reflection of Julian in demon form grinned back at him, yellow eyes twinkling, knowing secrets that Jack kept locked away. Jack collapsed, his face falling into the puddle causing the haunting image to dissipate.

CHAPTER 23

The heat of an open fire was the first thing that the semi conscious Jack felt, it was soothing and helped to dry out his sodden carcass. He stared into the dancing flames and realised he had been propped up in an armchair in front of the fireplace at The Old Cock Inn. A blanket had been wrapped around him, his clothes sat in front of him drying out, warm vapour rising up from his trousers and sweater. He imagined that this was just how he looked, steaming, like a pot of vegetables coming to the boil.

"He's coming round." He heard a voice say, it was deep and gruff, "I'll tell Mrs Crowfoot."

"Crowfoot!" Jack murmured and suddenly that was enough to bring him round, he realised where he was and what was happening. Jack turned to see a crowd of concerned faces gathered around in the pub, staring at him. Relief fell on some of those faces when Jack came too and tried to focus, his eye lids flicking rapidly as they adjusted to the light.

"I'm okay." Jack said instinctively and tried to stand up but withered back into his seat.

His eyes flitted across everyone's concerned gazes and then saw the landlady glaring at him, obviously not everyone looked relieved to see he'd come round. She looked like she had just eaten something sour, as she vigorously cleaned a glass tankard with her damp cloth.

Jack expected that the steam that was rising from his damp body was only half caused from the fire, the other fifty percent was surely being caused by her glare.

"So, you're finally awake!" Came the unmistakable cackle of Mrs Crowfoot.

"Mrs Crowfoot!" Jack said.

She shuffled slowly across the pub, her frailness causing her to clutch the arm of a large burly man, who steadied her and helped her towards Jack.

"Ah! Good to see that you have all your faculties, young Mr Heron."

The crowd parted to let them through, their respect for her was almost biblical and it reminded Jack of the story of Moses and the parting of the Red Sea. This image made Jack chuckle.

"And your sense of humour is still intact I see?" She smiled a jagged smile as she reached him.

Another large man slid out a chair for her and she slowly sat down facing Jack. She smiled, it was warming even though her mouth looked like a rockery.

"Joanie! Get him a Scotch!" She suddenly cried which caused the landlady to jump on the spot, interrupting her leering.

"But..." Joanie attempted to say but was immediately overruled.

"Now, Joanie! And make it a double, he looks like he could do with it!"

He smiled at her and nodded. With one glance from Mrs Crowfoot, the crowd and burley man disbanded, returning to their tables and games. Whoever this woman was she had the respect of the whole town.

"Now, do you want to tell me how you ended up facedown in a puddle in the middle of the street, young man?"

"I...I don't remember." Jack said shaking his head.

Mrs Crowfoot grunted, dismissing his answer.

"Poppycock! You remember... Oh, yes, indeed you do!"

Joanie waddled across and held out the glass, an inviting Scotch rippled in her shaking grip before his eyes. A hand appeared out from the blanket and he took it, thanking her, she immediately left, grumbling something under her breath.

"I really can't..." He started but Mrs Crowfoot shook her head.

"You drink a bit of that and I'll see if I can jog your memory."

Jack sipped. There was a pause, as she looked solemnly into the fire.

"It's that house."

Jack just looked at her.

"Haunted they say." She said turning to face him, her old withered face lit by the fire, its glow causing the lines in her face to shadow and look like disturbing long lacerations.

"I... I guess it is." Jack murmured, sipping his Scotch again. He couldn't actually believe that he had agreed with her but it was the only explanation for everything that had occurred, wasn't it?

"You've seen things there haven't you?"

Jack nodded.

"I thought as much. What have you seen?"

Jack thought of all the things he had seen and experienced in just a few days that had felt like a lifetime. The constant Rat-a-tat-tat of the door knocker, the blood dripping from the tap in his dream (If it

133

was indeed a dream), the withering corpse of his Father, the sexual perverse housemaid, Mr Fiddler and his shotgun, the demon Julian that tried to drown him in the pond, that dark harpy that screamed at him to 'Get Out' and then Black Jack. He shuddered.

"You wouldn't believe me if I told you, Mrs Crowfoot."
She sat back in her chair, this was accompanied by a loud creaking, Jack could not work out whether it was her ancient joints that sang in discomfort or whether it was the chair.

"No, I Probably wouldn't." She smiled, "But, wouldn't you sooner get it off your chest and tell me what you have seen?"
Jack thought about the question for a few moments, took a quick look around the pub to see if anyone was listening. They all seemed to be lost in their own conversations and gameplay now, even Joanie, the landlady stood laughing at the far side of the bar enjoying a conversation with the large man that helped Mrs Crowfoot earlier. He thought that he was probably responsible for carrying him in off the sodden streets of Cyfrinach pwynt y De. Jack didn't know whether he was more surprised that no one was listening in or that Joanie was laughing, as he didn't think she was even capable of such a feat of strength.

"You have my ear, Mr Heron. Nobody will intervene."
He took a large gulp of Scotch, it burnt his throat as it flowed down towards an almost empty stomach and it gurgled when it hit.

"Well, there..."
Suddenly Mrs Crowfoot lurched forward and grabbed his hand, Scotch spilt from his glass as she held his hand in hers. She seemed impatient and could no longer wait for him to speak, tears lined up on her sagging eyelids, seemingly ready to dive off any second.

"Tell me!" She whispered, "Did, did he look okay?"

Jack looked at her confused.

"Who?"

"Mr Fiddler, of course!"

The contorted brow of confusion was replaced by a wide eyed expression.

"How did you know?"

She released him and leant back in the chair again.

"Shame what happened to him, a terrible shame."

"What, What did happen?" He pried, not wanting to but needing to know.

She looked at him and for a second he saw anger in her old eyes, was it anger out of daring to ask such a question or anger for not knowing.

"Mr Fiddler worked for your Grandfather for many, many years. He tended his garden, helped at the stables and acted as gamekeeper." The anger seemed to have disappeared as she gazed into the fire again, almost as if she were reminiscing.

"He was a grumpy sod sometimes, but he was kind hearted under his gruff exterior. Damn hard worker too."

"I remember him."

"Do you?" She asked looking at him again.

"Little bits, yes, he was always kind to me as a child."

She stifled a laugh in her throat and turned back to stare into those flames that must have been painting a portrait of the past for her eyes only, in vibrant shades of yellow and orange.

"He was a good man. His name was dragged through the mud because of what happened at that house, because of silly boys

135

playing silly games!" She stared at Jack then and it was a glaring look like a vulture peering at a helpless antelope as it withers away to its death.

"What do you mean?" Jack asked, mixed up memories danced in his head, puzzle pieces yearning to be slotted into the correct place.

"Joe! Well, that's Mister Fiddler to you. He killed himself because of you bloody kids that's why!"
The tears came now and a few of the punters glanced over at her with protective looks on their faces but she waved them away and their gazes were gone.

"But, what..." Jack said confused, "What did I do?"
Mrs Crowfoot looked at him and shook her head.

"You did nothing. That was the problem. You did nothing, Jack."

"I don't remember? I... I don't know what you are talking about?" She laughed.

"The human mind is a curious thing isn't it?"

"What do you mean?"

"How we forget things or manipulate a memory or action to our own ideals."

"I still don't understand what you..."

"It was your fault that Joe killed himself!"

"What?" Jack cried, the pub did not bat an eyelid at his outcry that almost saw him drop his glass and spill from the confines of the armchair.

"You know what happened. Somewhere behind one of those closed doors in the back of your mind you know."

"I really don't!" Jack snarled, becoming very defensive.

"It's human nature, we all do it! You have chosen to forget what happened out of guilt."

"I..." That was all Jack managed, as the pieces of puzzle in his head were floating around and starting to fit together correctly, the memory, the true memory was beginning to form.

"You probably played that moment over and over in your head a million times and because it was indeed painful, your brain changed it slightly, shaping it to suit you. First there was the guilt and then you would need to change it slightly, until you tell yourself it wasn't your fault and you weren't to blame at all. Like taking a sheet of parchment paper and laying it over an image and tracing it but changing the things you don't like. In the end it creates a new picture, one that to your mind is the truth."

Jack sat in silence, his head playing out an account of that day and he remembered.

"Tag! You're it!" He heard the words as clear as day, Julian ran down the stairs of Heron House, Jack gave chase. Julian darted into the dining room and ran around the table, Jack arrived and now they looked at each other in a stalemate. Julian could not run because Jack had the doorway blocked and if Jack chased then Julian would surely escape.

"I've got you now, Julian!"

"No fair! You're always cheating!"

"How am I cheating?"

"You just are! I'm going to tell my mum that you're cheating."

"You're such a whiner, Julian! You take the fun out of everything."

137

As Jack was distracted, Julian made for the door, but Jack was alive to it an he tagged him on the back.

"You're it!" Jack yelled and ran off back down the corridor towards the kitchen.

"Bastard!" Julian yelled at the top of his voice, a petulant crease formed across his devilish brow.

"Now, now watch your language, Julian!" Came his mother's voice from somewhere upstairs.

Jack burst into the kitchen where Ms Soaper was elbow deep in washing up.

"Slow down, you heathen!" Ms Soaper said playfully.

Jack panted and looked around the kitchen for a place to hide, he contemplated hiding under the oak table, the red and white checkered table cloth hung down enough on one side to conceal him from Julian's gaze. He looked at Ms Soaper and she shook her head.

"You know he'll find you under there."

Jack danced about on the spot, rapidly losing hope.

"You're best off outside." She suggested with a wink.

Jack smiled and darted out of the open door into the courtyard. In the distance he saw Mr Fiddler tending to the flower beds with his gardening hoe in hand. Mr Fiddler greeted him with a wave. Jack looked around but could not decide where was best to go. He knew that he couldn't head for the stables as that was out off bounds in their made up world of tag, he didn't give the place a second thought anyway, not since that ordeal with Black Jack, he had not ventured up there since. He could hear Julian's whining drone as he pleaded with Ms Soaper to tell him where Jack had got too but she would not yield. He suddenly focused on the fountain and the pond, the statue of the hippocampus was his saviour. He smiled because he knew that Julian could not swim and he bounded forward towards it. He stepped over the side and into the pond, it came up to his neck, he remembered how cold the water was that day. Somewhere in the future an older version of Jack sits in an old Welsh pub shivering with the recollection of the waters chilly temperature. As he paddled through the water the prize winning koi carp brushed passed his legs as they swam. He made it to the monument in the centre and climbed up onto the ledge at the foot of the hippocampus, where a large stone fish tail protruded. He hid behind it so that when Julian came out of the kitchen he would not see him.

"Hey, Jack! Where are you?" Julian shrieked as he burst into the garden.

Mr Fiddler turned around to see what the commotion was and could see Jack crouched behind the large hippocampus. Jack put his fingertip to his lips and Mr Fiddler winked and smiled, before returning to his duties. Water spat out of the top of the fountain and spluttered, the falling water helped to conceal Jack even more, he watched as Julian stood with his hands on his hips and his chest heaving in and out as he looked around for his missing cousin.

"No fair, Jack! No fair!" Groaned Julian.

Jack couldn't hold in his suppressed laughter and he spat out a cackle. That was all Julian needed and now he was on to him, he ran up to the small wall of the pond that surrounded the fountain and it came up to his chest. Jack peered around the corner to see Julian's cross face staring back at him.

"No fair, Jack! You're a cheat!"

139

"I'm not cheating. Come and get me!" Jack mocked, knowing that Julian wouldn't dare because he couldn't swim. Jack had glanced back to see if Mr Fiddler was sharing in his delight that he had indeed got one over on his younger cousin this time. Mr Fiddler was higher up the garden, nearly on top of the hill that lead towards the stables now, investigating a loose beam on the fence. He turned his attentions to the kitchen window to see if Ms Soaper was there to flash him a wink at outsmarting the devious Julian but all he saw was her large backside disappearing out of the kitchen with a tray containing the family heirloom of one pristine *Royal Doulton* tea set.

"Alright then!" Julian said and was suddenly up on the side of the fountain and tightrope walking his way around, trying to get to him, he could not of course as Jack was in the centre of the fountain.

"Now you just be careful, Julian!" Jack warned.

"Don't be a dickhead, Jack!" Julian scowled. His language for one so young was foul but his mother never reprimanded him for it, she just always used to say, 'He gets it from his Father, the naughty boy' and then usually laugh and hug him. Julian was indeed a spoilt unpleasant brat but he still didn't deserve what happened next. Julian slipped and hit his head on the side of the pond before falling into the cold water. The sound of the splash replayed again and again in Jack's head as Julian's unconscious body floated facedown on the surface of the water.

Jack remembered calling out for help but remained frozen to the stone hippocampus, terrified to let go. He remembered a frantic Mr Fiddler with his hoe in hand trying to pull him towards him, however it was too late. He remembered Jack's Auntie Dilys running out of the house screaming at Mr fiddler, slapping at his shocked face and laying into him before gathering up Julian's sodden dead carcass and rocking it in her arms shouting at Mr Fiddler. She screamed at Jack asking what happened and if Mr Fiddler did this to Julian. Jack remembers looking at Mr Fiddler who looked shocked and was obviously only trying to save the poor boy. Jack felt in a daze and couldn't understand what was happening but then other family members and servants poured out to see what was happening and she frantically screamed at Jack if Mr Fiddler was responsible. Jack remember's Mr Fiddler's face fall as if a part of him had died when Jack slowly nodded his head. Having allowed this memory to finally replay in his minds eye, Jack could see now what had happened and why his Auntie Dilys had thought that Mr fiddler was to blame, from her vantage point, (possibly from a window high up in the house it looked as though he was pushing Julian down into the water and holding him there). Jack doesn't remember why he nodded though and allowed poor Mr Fiddler to take the blame for this. He may have been so traumatised by the whole ordeal that he didn't know what he was agreeing too or a part of him maybe did it instinctively, hoping that it would end the ordeal.

"Oh good God!" Jack gasped, the remaining Scotch lapped up the inside of the glass in his quivering hands, he downed it and fell back into the armchair with a wide-eyed expression on his face.

"A revelation can be a very disturbing experience, can it not?" Mrs Crowfoot asked, but Jack was unable to reply.

"Joanie! Bring him another double."

There was silence between the two as the drink was prepared and Joanie marched over and swapped the empty glass in his hand for a

141

new drink, he thought he said thank you but he wasn't sure, he wasn't sure about anything now.

His glass jittered up and down and back and forth, it clinked off his teeth as he struggled to sip it.

"I should have said something! I..." He sighed and felt so much guilt.

"Yes, you should have. What happened to Joe was needless. If you'd have spoken up he would still be with us."

"How did he die?"

"After firstly being wrongly accused of murdering a child, he was finally let go by the authorities who had said that you were seeing a psychiatrist at the time and were not of sound mind."

"Psychiatrist? No, that can't be right."

"That's what the police said." She shrugged, "Those quacks have ways of making you forget things though, probably hypnotised you to forget the ordeal to be honest. Can't say I blame them though. That's not the kind of thing for a child to see."

"Then how did he die?"

"The damage was already done. The blame, the guilt! He too had assembled his own reconstruction of events and played it over in his mind so much that he believed it was his fault, and that he should have been able to save the poor child."

Tears began to cascade down Mrs Crowfoot's hagged face, disappearing into the caverns that streaked across her cheeks.

"He was my betrothed. We were to be married, but he never recovered from that and he took the shotgun one day and..." With that she grabbed the double Scotch that was cradled in Jack's grip and downed it in one quick gulp.

142

"Get him another double!" She yelled, hoarsely.

Jack hung his head in shame, his eyelids now homing the build up tears.

"I'm so very, very sorry." She touched her sharp witch like fingertips to his chin and manoeuvred his head, they met eye to tear filled eye and she smiled.

"I forgive you."

"What! But, how can you?"

"You said sorry for one."

"But, surely..."

"I've been waiting here in this crumby old town for you to return for over twenty years!" She interrupted as Joanie slipped another glass into his mitt.

"For you to say those exact words. Granted I knew when all this happened you were a child and not really to blame for any of it, and that is something that you must tell yourself before this is all over, if you want to move on with your life, that it wasn't your fault really."

"But I hadn't..."

"Bah!" She interrupted, sitting back in her chair, as relaxed as he had seen her over the past few meetings, "Guilt is made up of 'Buts' and 'What ifs'! Life isn't like that, you can't change what has happened, so you have to just move on with your lives. That's what I did, I was bitter and angry for so long while I waited for you to return."

"How did you know I would return?"

"I knew. You're human and the past has a way of catching up with you, no matter how far you try and run away from it. That is

143

why you are best just facing it. I woke up one day and told myself that. I've been a lot happier since I did, I can tell you that much!"

"Well, I am glad you accept my apology."

"I guess you should go back there now and say it to Joe too. Only then will your conscience truly be cleansed."

"Yes, and to the others..." He said trailing off into the corridors of his own mind, to see if there are other doors that he has closed that needed to be reopened.

"Beg your pardon? Others?"

"Never mind, just a slip of the tongue."

CHAPTER 24

Jack found himself in front of Heron House again, after a long emotional embrace with Mrs Crowfoot. Jack had got dressed and bid her farewell. She had insisted that one of the patrons drive him back to the house and see him safely to the door. The burly man that Jack had seen helping her earlier gave him a lift in a dilapidated Ford Escort and conversation was brief, mostly about the weather. He informed Jack that there was indeed another storm on the way, he said he could smell it in the air.

The man had left him at least fifteen minutes ago, but Jack still remained in the same spot, his toes squelching in his shoes as rain hammered down, leaving him wet through again. His wet hair slid down his slender face, covering his eyes and the moist tips kissing his protruding cheekbones. He still did not move. That Welsh breeze returned, surrounding him again like some hurricane, he felt for a moment that the wind would actually lift him off the ground, that his sodden feet would scrape against the gravel underfoot as he was elevated into the air. The wind moved on, seemingly no longer having any interest in him and began to attack the trees on the horizon that were dotted around by the stables. A horse neighed in the distance, he closed his eyes and thought of Black Jack. The door knocker rattled back and forth with its usual haunting rhythm. The wind brought with it voices, whispering 'Get Out' and giggling that even while he was standing in front of the house in the middle of a rainstorm it made him feel embarrassed and inferior. He tilted his head back, his hair flopping away from his face and hanging behind him like dark swollen leeches that had had their fill. He felt the rain ricochetting on his face. His eyes remained closed and he felt the rain trickling down his face and seep into his clothes. He felt as though he was submerged, it was a claustrophobic sensation as though trapped in a tank like some illusionist or escape artist, as it filled slowly with water, but for Jack there seemed to be no escape. He felt like he was floating in this narrow tank, something tugging on his legs, tearing at his trousers, Julian yearning for Jack to join him. Then something pushing down on top of his head with great force. In his mind he saw Mr Fiddler, half of his face removed by a close range shotgun shell, pushing him down with his garden hoe. Then he opened his mouth and exhaled, there was no tank of water, no Mr fiddler, no Julian, just the rain that relentlessly lashed down in sheets. The wind was back again in a wave bringing with it this time a familiar sound, a gut wrenching and distressing sound, a groan of his dying Father. Jack's heart seemed to become tight as though it were being squeezed in gigantic hands. Was this a heart attack he thought? Is this how it all ends? But no, it was another panic attack. He swallowed hard and the terrifying groan disappeared and so did the uncomfortable vice like grasp around his rapidly beating heart. The rain started to feel strangely warm and uncharacteristically thick, syrupy globs fell on his eye lids, the rain had changed, it brought with it a familiar smell. It fell onto his lips and seeped into his mouth, his tongue tasted it, it was almost metallic and it stimulated his gag reflex causing him to retch and dry heave. All around him all these mental plagues seemed to be on him all at once, taking from him like a swarm of thirsty mosquitoes. His chest grew tight, his head hurt, his heart rate increased dangerously. In his stomach nausea was being concocted that would be ready to serve up in the next few seconds, but before the vomit could rise in his throat, he opened his eyes again and it all stopped. Jack looked around, in the distance he saw a flash of lightning and a grumbling of thunder and with the rain still attacking him he crunched his way through the gravel towards the house. His face seemed determined, like there was something he must do. He entered the house without giving a second thought for that black iron stallion that rattled on the door.

CHAPTER 25

Jack had devoured yet another tin of baked beans, and was on his way towards the hallway. He was actually moving freely around the house and had done a terrific job of blocking out the things that terrified him about the place. He had grabbed his cellphone, but unfortunately there was still no signal and a minuscule amount of battery left now, indicating only 10% left. He made his way into the study and plugged in the phone to charge again. Unfortunately this time it blew the fuses and the house was plunged into darkness, all apart from the dying embers in the fireplace.

"Oh, shit! Just what I need."

Those gruesome terrors scratched at the doors that Jack had closed on them, trying to keep them contained and not have to face them, trying to ignore and forget them. He heard them, in the dark things always seem ten times worse, shadows play tricks on the mind but the mind doesn't help, it is fickle and believes the lies that the darkness displays, even his eyes started to believe its constant lies.

"There's no need to be afraid of the dark. There is nothing in the dark that isn't in the light." He stopped for a moment pondering that sentence, that was something his Father used to say to him when he was very little. He thought of his Father alive and strong, sitting on his bed comforting him, it was a pleasant memory and a nice feeling. He switched the flashlight on his phone and hurried over to the fire where he stoked it and added more lumps of coal and sparking it into life once more. Soon the room was bathed in its warming glow and it didn't seem so scary anymore. He watched as the flames reflections flickered on the Wall of Champions, it seemed to make each horse prance or move in some way. Feeling a little more positive now he ventured out into the hallway. He quickly skipped across the cold floor, again his feet bare and finally free of sodden shoes and socks, he opened a small cupboard under the stairs. The small nook was musty and covered in thick sticky cobwebs, he shone the flashlight into the darkness and found the fusebox fixed to the wall. It looked ancient and retired like it had never actually ever worked, he flicked switches but nothing happened.

He was to have no electricity tonight.

"I won't let whatever these feelings are deter me from what I am going to do." He felt what he said to be the truth, yet he didn't really believe it and that was the problem.

"I'm going to carry on with what I was going to do!" He said firmly, following the bright white beam of his cellphone flashlight into the hall and to the foot of the stairs, not even looking at the silhouette of the figure through the window of the front door.

"I'm going to go and run a bath, then have another drink and go to bed!" The beam of light shone up the stairs as he trudged up them, shadows playfully mocked him with their scampering across the walls. Reaching the landing he slowly followed the long corridor towards the family bathroom, there would be no naked French maids in there to scalp his libido.

"Tomorrow this will all be over. I can sign the papers and be gone from this infernal place."

He tried not to focus on the doors that behind hoarded those grim sights, his Father's rotting corpse and that floating, shrieking hag. He kept focussed and followed the light. Quickly he found the bathroom and disappeared inside, closing the door behind him with some urgency. He stripped off and disposed of his clothes that were now good for nothing. After being soaked through on a number of occasions today, so much so that they had been left misshapen.

"Hopefully there is enough hot water in the tank to at least let me have a hot bath."

He turned the tap, it screeched and whined. It was obvious that it had not been used in some time. With a spluttering coughing fit the tap sprang into life and the steaming hot water burst out into the cast iron bath, much to Jack's satisfaction.

"Well, at least that's something." He said and wondered over to the airing cupboard to see if there were any towels, there were a couple sitting in a nice neat pile, a layer of dust on the top one. Jack slid the bottom one out and unravelled it, he shook it and small flecks of dust escaped and evaporated into the air. The towel was a little bit stiff but it would suffice. He checked his cellphone and realised that the flashlight was rapidly draining the battery life so, feeling brave he turned off the flashlight to try and conserve some energy. He thought that the gentle glow from the phone's screen was ample light for his bathing.

"Candles!" He cried, his voice echoing over the running of the water, "There always used to be candles and matches in the airing cupboard."

He was soon back again in the airing cupboard and pulling out an old shoe box, in it were various used candles of different shapes and sizes, which were accompanied by a box of matches. An old lady dressed up in victorian garb was drawn on the box with the words *Phyllis' Matches* stamped on, in an olde word style font. As warming vapour rose around him, he struck the match and lit the candle, placing it on a chair that now homed his cellphone. The glow was soothing and turning off the tap just as the water had started to run cold he slid into its calming embrace. He sank down into it, exhaling in a moment of relaxation, probably the first real moment like this since he had been here. He closed his eyes and felt the heat surround him, at first it was a shock to the system then his body became used to it, but now it seemed to be too hot, it was stifling him. He sat up and turned the tap back on, adding some cold water as he lay back down. He closed his eyes and was again met by a vision, he was running down a corridor, not much different to the ones in this house and doors were opening on both sides. Jack darted to and fro slamming the doors shut again but they just kept on opening, until he bolted up right in the bath. The bathtub was overflowing now and he clambered to turn the tap off.

"Bloody hell!" He sighed, lying back down.

The sound of water falling from the tap and into the bath water was all that could be heard and he watched the droplets form and then fall away until something strange started to happen. Blood started to trickle out of the spout and then came in thick clotted lumps filling the bath. Jack felt frozen with fear and his stomach turned over in disgust, as he now lay in a bath of blood.

"Oh my God! Oh my God! What is this?"

He sat up trying to back out of the bath and as his knees spread something rose from between them. He sat in a puddle of his own fear as a naked woman stood up out of the thick plasma, she was covered in blood from her head to her toes, breasts small and pert. He watched in horror as crimson drips fell from her nipples and dotted his face.

"Good God!" He shook as he realised it was his Auntie Dilys. She stared at him with black eyes, the sockets caked in a thick layer of blood, they were not forgiving eyes.

"Auntie Dilys!" He stuttered.

Her arms hung by her sides and her fists clenched tightly, blood oozing out of the gaps in her fingers.

"What do you want from me, for God sake!" He cried. She unclenched her fists and turned her hands around to show her inner arms and the wounds on her wrists. Heavy hacks were carved into each wrist, tendons and bone exposed but eerily no blood seeped from the wounds. There was no more blood for her to give. She suddenly sank back down into the bloody water and disappeared, the plasma lapped up the sides of the bath and out of it, smearing the linoleum floor red. Jack scrambled to get out of the bath but was pulled down into the crimson liquid. Underneath it felt so deep and she entwined herself around him, hands at his throat choking at him as he gasped for air and kicked to get free. His lungs were being starved of oxygen and he started to conjure up images of Julian and she let go of him. He burst through the surface of the water and clambered out of the bath and fell onto the floor in a puddle of water and blood like a newborn. He slid on his backside away from the bath and grabbed at a dressing gown that hung on the bathroom door. He dropped it over himself cowering under it as his wide eyes were fixated on the bath. Sure enough she rose from it again like a mythical kraken, blood spraying everywhere in her furious wake. She started to come for him again.

"Julian!" He screamed at her and much to his surprise she stopped.

"It wasn't my fault Auntie Dilys!"
She snarled and came for him again.

"I'm sorry!"
Still she came, eyes black and furious. He thought that that might have worked, why did she want him if he wasn't to blame. Before she could come closer he managed to get to his feet and burst out of the bathroom. He tied the robe around him and fled down the stairs, and into the hallway where he skidded and nearly slipped over, his feet still sodden.

RAT-A-TAT-TAT! Erupted from the other side of the door and Jack could take no more!

"I wish you would bugger off!"
He cried and aggressively flung open the door.

"Here I come with a rat-a-tat-tat!" Said a familiar voice as lightning sliced outside revealing his Grandfather standing in front of him. Jack collapsed in an exhausted faint.

CHAPTER 26

Jack woke up slouched on the armchair in the study, the warm glow of flames lapping at his exposed flesh. The robe was in disarray, covering his modesty but not a lot else. His scrawny frame was exposed and the shadows caused by the fire's radiance were not complimentary, it made him appear gaunt and almost skeletal. He rubbed at his head, sick and tired of everything now. He was at the end of his tether and did not think he could bring himself to spend another night in this wretched house. He kept his eyes closed and sunk back in the chair, he sighed and asked himself what more did he have to do? He had tried to shut these sights out and it had seemed to work for a short time. Yet there seemed to be more horrors awaiting him. The sight of his Auntie Dilys lathered with crimson was the stuff of nightmares, a vision he believed would never vanish from his mind and would haunt him for the rest of his days. A breeze crept in and the flames shivered against it, Jack mimicked the flames and pulled the robe around him properly. His fingertips caressed something on the breast pocket. He opened his eyes as he looked down at what it was, and protruding out of the burgundy silk were the hand stitched initials 'W.C.H' in beautiful calligraphy.

"William Cyril Heron. Grandad." Jack whispered as he ran his fingers over the letters. He smiled and pulled the robe to his face and inhaled. His Grandfather's scent still remained and it was very comforting. The scent was so strong that all those memories flooded back of his time spent with him, they were happy memories and he let them surge in as if cleansing all the lurid delusions that had manifested in his subconscious. It was amazing to him that how one positive interaction could disperse the clouds of negativity.

"I must harness this positivity and try to remember more of the good times. Enjoy the people I love more and collect the positive experiences to replay in my mind. Surely that's the way to extinguish the negativities?"

"You've hit the nail on the head there, Jack." Came a gravelly voice. Jack's eyes looked up and he bolted upright with an incredible scream. The sound of his shriek carried out into the hall and up the stairs, it was probably even enough to frighten that thing in his Mother's room, or maybe not.

"I do wish you wouldn't keep doing that." Said his Grandfather who sat opposite him on an almost identical armchair, "Goes right bloody through me."

"G-Grandad!" Jack stammered staring at him as he tried to scramble up the wing of the armchair.

"Stop messing about and sit yourself down, lad." His Grandfather said with impatience. As if automatically programmed into Jack's psyche, he did as he was told and slid back down into a seated position, his eyes still wide trying to analyse what he was actually looking at. Sat in front of him with two glasses of Scotch gripped in his hands was his Grandfather, William Cyril Heron, dressed in his best Sunday suit (he always dressed well, even if there was no occasion to be had, he always made the effort), A burgundy

155

tie smartly tightened up in a half Windsor knot underneath a pristine white collar. A matching burgundy pocket square flowered out of his breast pocket in a less formal puff fold. While underneath his medals hung proudly, metallic stars and coins dangling from multicoloured ribbons, glistening magnificently in the fire's fluorescence.

"But...You're dead!" He stuttered, swallowed hard and the words spewed out unceremoniously.

"Thanks for reminding me." Chuckled his Grandfather.

"Here have a drink." He added and handed him one of the chunky crystal cut glasses.

Jack took the glass in a shaking hand and started to gulp at it.

"Hey now! Calm down! You don't treat Scotch like that! Sip it for goodness sake, lad."

Jack did and stared at his Grandfather who sat smiling at him, tears assembled on his eyelids preparing an escape.

"I don't understand this." Jack whimpered, "I don't understand any of this!"

"Come on now, lad. Don't get upset. I'm here to help you, that's all. Surely you're not scared of your old Grandad! Are you?"

"Fucking terrified!"

His Grandfather let out an explosion of laughter and slapped at his thigh like some pantomime hero.

"Oh, I can hear your Auntie Dilys now!" He boomed, "'Now watch your language'" He mimicked in a not very convincing female voice.

Jack somehow calmed and seemed to be settled by his Grandfather's spectral presence.

"Well, I'm glad you finally let me in."

"That was you all this time?"

"Of course it was! You mean you don't remember the knock?"

"The knock?"

"My knock!"

Jack looked at him through a furrowing brow of confusion, but the cogs turned somewhere deep in the back of his mind, something familiar yearning to seep out.

"I don't believe it! You forgot the knock!" His Grandfather said with a disappointing shake of his head.

"Here I come..." Murmured Jack.

"With a Rat-a-tat-tat!" His Grandfather finished, "Yes!"

"Of course!" Jack said smiling, memories of his Grandfather returning home and that playful rhythm tapped out on the door knocker as the words joined it, his unmistakable gruff voice announcing he was home.

"I would have been here sooner but you wouldn't let me in!" He chuckled.

"Sorry!" Jack said, actually smiling now, "Rat-a-tat-tat! That was driving me mad! It all makes sense now."

"Does it?" His Grandfather asked with a hint of cynicism.

"Well, not really. None of it does! But, at least I know where the Rat-a-tat-tat comes from."

"Indeed!" Smiled his Grandfather.

There was a pause as Jack searched for the best way to put his next question. In the end he just blurted it out.

"So are you a ghost?"

"Ha!" His Grandfather shouted and shook his head in disbelief, "Is that what you think this is, Jack? A haunted house?" Jack shrugged, slightly embarrassed as he felt his grandfather was mocking his ordeal.

"Then what is this? Because I tell you, I'm ready to pack up and get the hell out of Dodge!"

"Take it easy. I'll tell you because that is what I am here for. A part of me thought you might understand if you spent a few days here, but alas it has been too long and the wounds have indeed been dressed with layer upon layer of bandage to stop the seepage of such terror."

"I don't understand."

"I know. That is why I am here, lad. Too many years have passed and you have blocked it out. Blocked it all out, your past and your childhood, most of your existence and your own family. The pain I agree was considerable, but I go to my grave being free and clear of conscience. I never once shied away from what happened. I faced it and it made me a stronger person, and a happier person in the end. I was not tormented or indeed haunted by the past for I wouldn't allow it. I grieved, yes, but I never once blamed myself for these atrocities. None of it was my fault and it wasn't yours either. That is what you need to realise. That is why you are here, Jack."

Jack felt the words of his grandfather working around his system but he still was having trouble connecting all the dots. He still didn't understand. It was as though something was impeding his Grandfather's words.

"I..." Jack murmured, shaking his head and emotion swelling up around the dark sockets that circled his eyes.

"Looks like we may be here a while then, lad. Best have a drink."

Jack did as he was told and managed to fight back the tears from all the confusion. His Grandfather took a long sip as if to wet his whistle for an epic citation.

"Are you trying to tell me that this place isn't haunted? But that I am!" Jack asked.

"Kind of."

"What do you mean, 'kind of'?"

"You are haunted, but not by ghosts."

"Then by what exactly?"

"Fear."

They both looked at each other, neither of them blinking. If there were no ghosts then how was his deceased Grandfather sitting in front of him telling him all of this? His brain felt tight as though his skull was closing in on it.

"You're asking yourself questions aren't you, Jack? But they are not the right questions."

"I don't understand, Grandad." He whined, his head in pain and tears trickling.

"It is fear, Jack. That's all it has ever been. However I believe that for it to sink in, then we must dissect the whole ordeal. Throughly!"

CHAPTER 27

"Fear is the word, Jack." His Grandfather said after clearing his throat.

"Fear? Of what?" Jack queried.

"Oh, it can come in many forms, and from these seeds of fear, these afflictions can grow. And I'm not just talking about fear of water, or of horses. Fears that you wear like a sandwich board around your neck but of the hidden ones as well. Those that you keep locked away in the back of your mind."

"Locked away." Whispered Jack, that resonated with him, something rung true.

"Yes, Jack." Nodded his Grandfather, "You have tried to suppress these feelings by locking them away behind closed doors, which you have in turn locked and chained!"

"But, what..."

"Anxiety, paranoia, guilt, low self-esteem." He paused, cleared his throat and added, "Sexual inadequacy."

Jack's glance fell to the floor and watched as his long toes dance nervously as his face was slapped with a flush of beetroot.

"These are the poisons that were originally concocted in this house when you were younger, these are the demons that you have been hoarding and that is not healthy. Sooner or later they are set free and that is the beginning of the end. You have never spoken of these feelings have you?"

"No." Jack murmured with embarrassment.

"This is why these manifestations are so strong, so very powerful. You have never faced them. You chose to ignore them, pretending they weren't there, believing that if you did that they would just go away. You've harboured them in the back of your mind for so long that it's made you forget the life you once had, because the bad memories were too painful, so you blocked it all out. These demons have grown stronger, waiting for the right moment, when your defences are down."

His Grandfather took a sip of Scotch, and Jack thought how could figments of his imagination drink Scotch.

"My death was the catalyst, it stirred them. Returning home was the trigger, being in familiar surroundings these fears escaped to wreak havoc."

Jack visualised all these fears in the forms of all these inner demons breaking through doors and seeping out of the orifices in his head, his ears, his nostrils, his mouth. Their ghastly forms dancing around in the air like fireflies before dispersing into the crannies of Heron House, to the place they would do the most harm and be the most effective.

"How do I..." Jack said, but the tears fell and his head dropped again.

"I wish," His grandfather sighed, "...that I could console you, Jack. I would give anything to be able to embrace you and tell you everything was going to be okay, but I can't. Maybe that is something that should have been done a long time ago by your

Mother, and if the truth be told by me. You never used the most powerful tool at your disposal, you never spoke up, or told anyone. A problem shared and all that."

"But, how could I have? Mother didn't... She wouldn't..." He sighed, "She was too consumed with Dad's death."

"Then there was always me, you could have spoken to me."

"I... I was scared."

"The fear!" He nodded, "It runs through everyone's veins, my lad, but sometimes you have to ask yourself what are you actually afraid of? What's the worst thing that can happen if you share your thoughts and feelings? To be judged? If you are judged for sharing such intimate details by your chosen trustee then does the fault not lie with them? Not with you! Are they really to be trusted in the first place? If they love you they will stick by you and love you no matter what and if they choose not to, then I guess they were merely acquaintances and nothing more."

Jack seemed to take a long time mulling his Grandfather's statement over, all the while his Grandfather just sipped at his Scotch and waited for a reply.

"It's a lot of information to take in all at once." Jack said, "But..."

"No!" His Grandfather interrupted shaking his head, "There's no 'But' in this scenario, Jack. You're telling yourself to put up the defences, the way that it as always done when you've had to think of these things that hurt. Or when things get tough and you can't face them. Instead of facing them or asking for help!"

"It's not a cry for help." Jack scoffed.

"And that is denial. You are asking for help but when help is offered, or a way around such difficulties you don't take it. Sooner or later that help will not be there. Can you fight these inner demons alone? Would you even want to?"

Jack didn't know what to say but he knew that this is something he had been guilty of his whole life. He had never dealt with any of his problems and even when he had been obviously stressed about something or expressed help (in a round about way) he never took any of the advice from people he called friends, like Marcy.

"Marcy." Jack murmured.

"Yes, Marcy, she has always been there for you and offered a helping hand that you have never taken. Instead you close up when you should be taking the advice given. People who do that become martyrs."

"I love her. Marcy, I love Marcy!" Jack beamed with realisation.

"About time you figured that out." His Grandfather chuckled.

"I must tell her, I must see her..." Jack said excitedly rising from the chair looking around for the cell phone that was indeed still of no help to him and currently residing in the upstairs bathroom that Jack visualised being covered in blood by now.

"First things first lad." His Grandfather said which seemed to stop Jack in mid-stride and he sat back down.

"But, I..."

"No, we need to talk it all through first."

Jack took another sip of Scotch and waited on his Grandfather again.

163

"I want you to close your eyes and tell me what you see in your mind's eye." Jack closed his eyes and his eyelids fluttered frantically as if fast asleep in the midst of some nightmare.

"I see lots of things, everything! It all just whizzes past like traffic."

"Pick one thing out."

"Auntie Dilys! Auntie Dilys covered in blood, rising out of the bathtub and coming for me."

"Why is she coming for you?"

"She blames me for something. I think she wants to kill me!"

"Do you remember what happened to Auntie Dilys?"

"No."

"She committed suicide."

Jack remained silent, his Adam's apple forcing its way down his throat as if swallowing an oversized pill, it rose again and his lips quivered as if he were about to cry out.

"Do you remember, Jack?"

"Yes!" He sobbed.

"You found her, remember?"

Jack nodded.

"Tell me what you saw."

Jack sniffed and a string of mucus was inhaled back into the safety of his nostril.

"She was lying in the bathtub, the water was red... it was blood." He gulped again, "Her arm hung out of the bath, a razor lay on the linoleum in a..." Jack started to choke up.

"Go on. You can do it."

"A puddle of blood! Her blood, she had slit her wrists."

"Yes." His Grandfather replied with a sigh of remorse.

"The blood dripped from the wound. Her fingers seemed to have formed a point and blood dripped from her finger where she had managed to write the letter 'J' on the floor. Her eyes were open. Goddamn those glazed eyes stared into my soul! They blamed me for Julian! That was what the 'J' was for! She was going to spell out my name and shame me! Blame me!" He threw his hands over his teary eyes and shook like the petal on a flower caught in the midst of an April shower.

"It was my fault!"

"No." His Grandfather murmured.

Jacks hands slid down from his moist face and he stared at his Grandfather.

"No?"

"No, Jack. Dilys was a mess after Julian died. Sunken into a depression that was irreversible. We tried everything to help her, the best psychiatrists money could buy but nothing could bring her back. She was broken and had given up. You see what I mean about being too far gone?"

Jack nodded.

"She had let it consume her and she had passed the point of no return. I know from personal experience that she never once blamed you for what happened Jack."

"Really?"

"Really, I listened to her recordings with the psychiatrist. Never once did she mention your name in a negative light. If anything she blamed herself, that is the case in most suicides. The victim thinks that it is all their fault and the only way to deal with that guilt is to say goodbye."

"But, the 'J' on the floor? And why was she coming for me like that!"

"The 'J' probably stood for Julian. I'm certain of it."

"Of course!" Jack gasped, but his face looked a little brighter, "How could I be so arrogant to believe it meant me."

"A picture can tell a thousand words but sometimes they are the wrong words."

"Meaning?"

"It was a very traumatising experience for you and you were young for one! Like most youngsters their world is small and they think that everything revolves around them."

Jack blushed a little embarrassed.

"Don't be ashamed, every child thinks this because in a way they are! They are the centre of the universe for their parents and family bends over backwards to accommodate their whims and fancies. So naturally they grow up with a narcissistic complex that life is all about them. It's not until later on in life that most grow out of this and understand that we are all just as important as them"

"Then why was she coming for me?"

"I don't know." Shrugged his Grandfather taking another sip of his drink, "Maybe she thought you were Julian and just wanted a hug. She obviously didn't get to finished her goodbye message that she had been planning."

"Is it possible that this could all just disappear if I confronted it?"

"Yes, I do! This is what I am trying to get into that thick skull of yours." He answered in jest, "It can all be put to bed, but you need to know each demon's reason first."

"It was my guilt then I guess."

"Yes, you have carried your own guilt and hers for all these years. It's time to let go of that guilt."

Jack nodded.

"But, guilt from this particular ordeal is also anchored to other demons I feel."

"Julian?"

His Grandfather nodded, "And Mr Fiddler."

"Yes, Yes of course!" Jack seemed enthusiastic but still sick to his stomach, his Grandfather had been right in what he had said so far though, that talking about things and sharing them was very cleansing.

"You obviously remember fully what happened to Julian, you have probably relived it a million times over!"

"Oh, God yes!"

"And do you still blame yourself for what happened?"

"I... No, No I don't. It was an accident."

"Exactly, my lad!" His Grandfather said smiling proudly.

"I had hidden in that place hundreds of times. Julian just used to give up if I had managed to get there during our games. So I guess it was..." Jack paused not wanting to say the next words.

"His fault?" His Grandfather managed to finish his sentence for him.

"Well, yes I guess."

"You don't have to feel bad for that, it was his fault. No matter how much I loved Julian, he was a little bastard!"

"Grandad!" Jack gasped.

"Well, it's true, he was. Obviously I never wished any ill fate on the poor child, I loved him like my own, but he was stupid and stupid finds trouble sooner or later."

"Well, I guess. It just seems a bit harsh."

"Put it this way, do you think he felt any guilt or remorse over intentionally locking you in that stable with old Black Jack?"

Jack shook his head.

"No, he bloody didn't! The little shit!"

They both chuckled.

"But, seriously, no, he didn't deserve what happened to him but it was his own fault. Again not yours!"

"I think I am seeing that now. Probably why I have a fear of water now."

"Another fear to over come perhaps at a later stage?"

"Perhaps." He smiled, his eyelids were moist and although it was gut wrenching to talk about such terrible experiences, it was helping.

"Mr Fiddler though is a different kettle of fish, my lad."

"How so?"

"Well, your guilt for not speaking up is justified."

Jack dropped his head and nodded in agreement.

"That guilt is yours and yours alone. Can you remember?"

"Yes, he tried to help Julian. Tried with all his might but it was too late. In fairness I think Julian had already gone when Mr Fiddler intervened."

"Indeed, the coroner said that he died from a fractured skull. Because Fiddler... Joe, I'm going to call him Joe because he was my friend and he had done nothing wrong. He deserves the respect of being referred to by his given name."

Jack nodded again in agreement.

"It's that coroner report that saved him from a life sentence, but unfortunately for poor old Joe, the damage had already been done. He too lived with the guilt I imagine, with his good name being dragged through the mud he could take no more. Guilty or not, he ended it with that gun of his."

Jack's head dropped once more and tears fell again.

"I understand that was traumatising for you and you were in some kind of haunted trance by it all, I know you know he didn't do anything but try to help. Have you seen him?"

"Yes."

"What happened?"

"He tried to shoot me."

"Probably justified." He laughed. Jack joined him in his laughter through his river of tears.

"That's an apology you have to make."

Jack smiled, "Mrs Crowfoot said the same thing."

His Grandfather nodded.

They sat in silence for a moment or too, the storm raged on outside the house but they said nothing to each other. Jack sensed that his Grandfather was about to move on to another subject, a delicate subject that probably if being honest neither of them wanted to have.

"Limp noodle." His Grandfather said.

Jack felt all manner of emotions surge through his body, embarrassment, low self-esteem and hysterics. Just hearing his Grandfather say it deadpanned as he did, sounded ridiculous and a part of him (the embarrassed part) held back the laughter.

"That's what she called you, isn't it?"

"Yeah."

"She was a fine looking girl. Bet you got an eyeful though, huh?"

Jack was again embarrassed and fidgeted in his seat.

"Okay, I'll try not to embarrass you too much lad, but it is another fear that you have to address."

"Do I though? I mean I've done okay without it for this long."

"But you're missing out on a natural pleasure that is second to none lad. Surely you would like to take that lass, Marcy, in your arms and..."

"Of course I would!" Jack intervened, "Don't you think I haven't tried? Well, not with her but with others, I can never... well, you know."

"Yeah, I know. Again it's that fear rearing its ugly head. See how much these fears can effect your psyche?"

Jack nodded again.

"These fears are stopping you from having a full life. What she did was exploit a minor! These days it would be seen as abuse, and it was! I mean look what it's done to your libido!"

"I don't really have one."

"Exactly my point!"

"I thought for a time that I may have been homosexual. Not that there is anything wrong with that you understand. I was... am

170

attracted to women, but I just struggle each time I try to make things happen."

"Making each experience for you worse I'd wager? Making you feel even more sexually inadequate. Am I right?"

"Yeah."

"Truth of the matter is that you were just a kid back then, and of course you shot your load when a naked women touched you for the first time."

"Jesus, Grandad!" Jack laughed.

"Well, it's true! It's not the situation that effected you but what she did and how she belittled you. That's what has stuck in your claw. Again something else you'll have to face."

"What do you mean?"

"I'd rather call an end to that discussion, thank you." He said having a large swig from his glass.

"But, how can I..."

"That's something you will have to work out for yourself, lad." Jack sipped his Scotch and it was his turn to watch his Grandfather squirm in his chair. Jack smirked and realised how at ease he felt, a feeling that he had never noticed in his life before.

"You're a workaholic as well aren't you, Jack."

"Sorry?"

"You work too much."

"I guess." He shrugs, "That's what Marcy tells me anyway. Tells me I should slow down."

"She's right."

"She is? But my work, I need to carry on..."

His Grandfather shakes his head interrupting Jack's flow.

"The work will always be there, the creativity will always be there. You don't have to beat yourself up about having time off here and there and to experience other things."

"But, the public will lose interest in me if I drop off the radar."

"Not at all! If anything it will make your work more sort after as there will be less of it."

"Well, I guess there is some truth in that."

"Of course there is!" His Grandfather tutted, "Plus you have to ask yourself what you are doing it for? Is it for the money, fame and adulation?"

"Well, I…"

"Greed! It overshadows what the purpose is sometimes. You don't need any more money, you have enough to live comfortably for a couple of lifetimes over. No, it's not about money or publicity, that is not what art is about. It's about creating, first and foremost creating something for you! If they like it and want to buy it for obscene amounts of money, then that's up to them. The pride and satisfaction from a piece should be enough for you."

"You're actually right! I think I have gotten that caught up in it all, that I have forgotten what's important."

"Exactly."

"I can change that outlook, but does that have anything to do with fear?"

"Of course. It all stems back to when you were a child, do you remember?"

Jack closed his eyes.

"When you used to draw all the horses from the Wall of Champions. Do you remember?"

"Yes!" He gasped, visualising those drawings in crayon.

"Your Mother is to blame for your low self-esteem issues, your fear of rejection, that's what it all comes down to. Fear of rejection. That is the reason you work like a dog all the hours God sends, because you're afraid of being forgotten. That's why you never stop because of how your Mother used to treat you."

"I don't remember."

"Close your eyes. Think back. It's there."

Jack closed his eyes again and pictured himself as a very small child running to show his mother his drawings. Sorrow tugged at the corners of his mouth and forced it into a horseshoe grimace.

"She never paid attention to you or your work did she?"

Jack shook his head tears trickling again, his mouth quivering from sadness to anger in waves.

"She never looked at my drawings. She always dismissed them! I sometimes found them in the bin."

"I know. I used to fish them out and play holy hell to her. She never listened of course, because of the drinking. She was like her sister in that regard and too far gone for me to even try."

"You kept my drawings?"

"I sure did lad. They're in the top drawer of my desk over there." He flicked a hitchers thumb over his shoulder in the direction of the desk behind him.

"Wow! Thank you for that. You don't know what that means to me."

"I do." He smiled a knowing smile.

"I can't believe she did that to me."

"Don't blame her too much, she was dealing with her own demons, unfortunately you were too young to remember the woman that she was. Maybe there are some good memories in there somewhere, maybe they will flourish when you lose a little of that baggage."

"I hope so."

"Your Mother's actions gave you that first fear, the fear that your work isn't good enough and that people will hate it. A paranoia in a way, but it also gave you the passion to prove her wrong, I guess, because it's the one thing you have stuck at. Look how successful you have become because of it."

"Are you saying I should thank her for putting me through that?"

"In a way, yes! All the work you create has been born through your fears, you just haven't noticed or taken the time to connect the dots. Just move on to the next piece, so you haven't got to think about it."

"Bloody hell!" Jack cried shaking his head, the realisation of all his artwork over the years had been just what his Grandfather had said.

"Some say that everything happens for a reason and maybe certain peoples sacrifices and actions were the catalyst for your success."

Jack sat back in his armchair the leather creaking wildly. His shock and realisation was etched on his gaunt face, his mouth hanging wide, as he gently shook his head from side to side.

"She used to tell me to get out of her room!" The sentence seemed to slowly whisper out of his mouth as if it were gas leaking.

174

His Grandfather said nothing.

"She used to rip up my drawings."

The tears came again and flowed uncontrollably.

"She threw things at me! Slammed the door on me. She would scream at me." He wailed now, in floods of tears, this time his Grandfather did not intervene. It was up to Jack to connect the dots.

"...Get...Out!"

His hand fell over his gaping maw and couldn't believe that that creature was how he perceived his Mother.

"Oh, God! I only ever wanted her love and attention and to show my work to Dad, and she never would... Dad..." Jack's face contorted again, the anger was gone and what was left was pain.

"Dad... I wish I could have seen him and talked to him before he died. There was so much I would have said to him. I just want him to..."

"I know, I know. That's a conversation for his ears not mine."

"But, how? How can I change any of it? How am I supposed to do this?"

"There's only one way, Jack. You face the fear."

CHAPTER 28

Jack left his Grandfather sipping away at his Scotch in the safety of his study. Well, his Grandfather or manifestation, illusion or whatever he was that his mind had conjured up.

He now understood what he must do to end all this, what needed to be said and to who. It was a hard pill to swallow in some cases, the words 'I'm sorry' could be a struggle to leave ones lips on occasions. Does anyone really like apologising? Taking the time to say sorry for something, means that you did something wrong or made a mistake. The majority of the human race are incapable of owning up to their mistakes or admitting they are even at fault. Some people look into the mirror and see a reflection that is squeaky clean, unable to be wrong in any way, shape or form. In those cases it is always someone else's fault, never theirs. Jack adjusted and tightened the belt of his Grandfather's robe around him, as he tiptoed through the dark corridor that lead to the kitchen, while thinking all the time about what had to be done.

I know what needs to be done now. I now know what this whole bizarre situation has been about. It's within me, it's all just been within me.

He stepped into the kitchen, that didn't feel homely at all to him anymore. There was no warmth from the stove or equal warmth from Ms Soaper. The strange smells that used to mix in the air of carbolic soap, freshly baked bread or those excellent sausage rolls had all gone now. Just the dripping of the old mixer tap at the sink, its long slender swan like neck starting to rust in places, but still having enough energy left to sputter out the spasmodic droplets of water. Jack stood in the kitchen, his eyes fixed on the back door that lead into the garden, the courtyard, the fountain. The memory of running through that door on that day to hide from his cousin haunted him, hung over him like a black cloud. It would be the last day that he saw his cousin, well, alive anyway. It was difficult for Jack to remember him how he was now, after seeing the gruesome hellion emerge form that soup like consistency of the pond water.

How do I face that again?

He shook his head, doubt had crept into his mind now and the fear was trying to take over again, but he knew what had to be done.

No, Jack! You have to face this... It's not him. Julian is dead and you're fighting with whatever demon you've conjured up in his image.

Jack stepped forward and out into the courtyard. It was as black as pitch now, the storm had settled and the clouds seemed to be dispersing. It still pattered with rain slightly but Jack thought he could deal with that after everything he had already been through. Jack hoped that the dissolving of the storm was a metaphor for the departure of the poisonous parasites that had taken up lodgings in his mind. Luckily the moon started to glow through the breach in the clouds and acted as a spotlight on the proceedings. Jack stepped out into the courtyard and approached the fountain and its pond, his body shook. He did not know whether it was fear or the cold that caused him to tremble, his bare feet like blocks of ice on the unforgiving damp slabs.

"J-Julian!" He called, his voice crackling under the pressure. There was nothing, no movement in the dark green waters of the pond.

"Julian!" He hollered again, this time in a manner that was firm and authoritative.

The water appeared to remain the same, then slowly several bubbles started to form on the surface, erupting like little green fireworks, spraying emerald droplets into the air before joining the water again. It bubbled up faster and faster, exploding as soon as they arrived as though something was about to materialise. Then nothing and the bubbles disappeared completely.

"Julian! Goddam you!" Jack yelled but the water remained calm.

Jack sighed a heavy but uneven sigh. There was a clicking sound from behind him. A familiar sound that sounded like a metal door bolt locking into place. Jack turned around slowly, his quivering lips managed to murmur the word, "Julian?"

When he turned around he found himself looking down the business end of a shotgun, Mr Fiddler's shotgun.

"M-Mister..." Jack stuttered stepping slowly backwards towards the pond, "...F-Fiddler." The haggard face of Mr Fiddler glared at him through his one good eye, the other eye had long since departed the moment that shot was discharged from close range all those years ago. Fiddler wore two faces in fact. The flesh on the defective side drooped like the melting wax of a candle. It had seemed to form a grimace of anger and pain, one that had had twenty plus years to refine. The more human side of his face seemed

178

tired and wilted with sadness, tears dancing around his eyelid. Jack knew this wasn't real, he knew what had to be done but the mind believes what the eyes see. Even if the mind is responsible for the hallucination, it all felt too real to him when he looked down the barrels, his nostrils twitching, agitated by the smell of the shot that was concealed inside its dark crevices. Jack continued to back up but Fiddler matched each stride, skulking forward with his shotgun positioned to remove Jack's head. Jack was halted by the wall of the pond, its cold moisture like icy fingers stroking the exposed flesh of his calves. Fiddler's sunken half face seemed to take pleasure in having Jack cornered.

"Mr Fiddler..." Jack squeaked and then coughed slightly to clear his throat as if that gave him the courage to face him.

"I'm so very sorry."

Fiddler's mangled face contorted, like some sort of confused animal, the gun seeming to quiver in his grip, like the two sides of his personality were fighting against each other. The sad half of him drooping with the weight of his guilt, his demonic side spoilt with the pain and anger.

"Can you hear me, Mr Fiddler?"

His face quivered, scowled, shook and grimaced, all in rapid succession as festering puss and plasma dripped from the hollowed out cavern in his skull.

"I know you can hear me." Stammered Jack swallowing hard, but making that first important step forward, towards Mr Fiddler.Fiddler's eye widened with bewilderment, astonished that his prey was actually heading towards him. Jack stepped forward, no longer feeling the damp and cold on the soles of his feet, they slapped on the slabs as he approached the hunter. Fiddler's halved mouth, fallen on one side like a stroke victim, blubbered and blurted out words that were almost incoherent. Jack thought that it sounded like 'Stay back' or 'It's too late' or it may have been both. Jack reached out with a shaking hand and gripped the double barrel shaft. It felt cold in his hand, and was reminded of the cold and damp all around him, he shivered. Maybe it wasn't the elements that made him shake but the fact that the gun that he held in his grasp felt so very real.

The gun shook up and down and so did Jack's hand.

"I-I know this is a long time coming Mister Fiddler." Sighed Jack, lowering his glance, a little ashamed and battling to say the words.

"None of this was your fault. None of it!" Jack sputtered out and suddenly the rain clouds opened again and there was yet another torrential downpour. The pair stood looking at each other as they become caught in a flurry of rain, the droplets singing as they ricochetted off the barrels of the gun.

"I should have said something, I should have spoken up. I was scared." Jack said dropping his head again and tears filling up in his eyes now.

"I know now that being scared isn't an excuse. You were not to blame for any of this, all you did was try and save Julian and I should have told them that, I should have shouted it from the rooftops."

Mr Fiddler lowered the gun, pointing it at the ground, tears seeping from his one good eye.

"I'm so sorry, Mr Fiddler. I really am!"

Mr Fiddler looked at him and smiled a crooked smile and suddenly his demolished face started to regenerate around that smile.

"Mr Fiddler, I was wrong to block all of this out and allow you to take your own life over this. I shall carry the burden of my mistake for the rest of my life, but I want you to know that you are free! Free and innocent."

"You'll carry no burden for me, Lad." Mister Fiddler whispered and Jack looked into a full face that was beaming, a glowing light surrounding him, "Thank you for coming back, Jack." He added before disappearing with the rain.

Jack looked up at the sky, that was now empty of clouds. Stars winked at him like dancing fireflies. He smiled, he felt so good about things, like a weight being lifted off his back. He backed up and sat down on the wall that surrounded the pond and fountain.

"I should have done this years ago." He laughed.

Jack had not noticed that the bubbles on the surface of the pond had returned and the dark creature (that resembled Julian in some lights) had started to rise up out of the pond. Green sludge hanging from his scrawny and soaked corpse. Jack must have sensed his cousin's presence and turned around quickly.

"Julian?"

There was nothing there, the water was calm and Jack shook his head, realising he was just jumping at shadows now.

"Stop being silly now, Jack" He laughed.

A corpselike arm appeared from behind Jack, grabbing him around the neck and pulling him into the pond. Once again Jack found himself tangling with the demonic version of his deceased cousin, Julian. Those yellow eyes glowing vibrantly in the mirky waters. A sadistic smile was carved into its impish face, with only one thing on its mind. Death! Initially Jack had struggled trying to fight off the creature but this only seemed to make matters worse. So he stopped fighting and allowed himself to go limp in the catlike grip of his cousin. The creature's brow contorted in confusion around those evil eyes. The two of them floated underwater, their hair fluttering upwards towards the surface like a clew of wriggling worms trying in vain to escape. Small bubbles escaped their nostrils as each held their breath, a trail of bubbles rising up to the surface rapidly. Jack noticed that Julian had loosened his grip and then he let go entirely. They floated looking deep into each other eyes and Julian's eyes started to change colour, that luminous colour disappearing and being replaced by two brown dots, Julian's eyes. Those eyes looked full of fear and sadness. Jack had only seen Julian's eyes like that once and that was when he fell and hit his head on the pond wall that day. He was always so brave, braver than Jack could ever be, there was never any fear, until that day. These are the eyes that Jack saw looking back at him now. He took Julian's hand and held it in his, giving it a loving and gentle squeeze. Tears started to drip from Julian's eyes, down his cheeks and then evaporated into the pond water. Jack smiled at him and Julian looked perplexed. Now Jack knew that he was not to blame for Julian's death, it was only an accident but obviously the guilt had chipped away at him for years. It was an accident and that was all there was to it. Jack knew that the words sorry were not needed in this particular situation, because he didn't have anything to be sorry for. One thing he did regret was that he never showed his cousin how much he actually loved him, even if the majority of the time he was a complete arse. He was still his blood and he loved him. Jack pulled Julian in close and wrapped his arms around him, hugging him tightly. Julian's eyes enlarged like saucers and at first did not react, in all honesty even when he had been alive he would not have known how to react to such warmth and affection. His Mother loved Julian very much, but apart from the occasional ruffling of hair and pecks on the cheek, the love that he craved so much was sparse. Finally Julian wrapped his arms around Jack and the pair floated together in a charming embrace. Jack noticed that Julian had started to pull away and then suddenly let go. Julian was sinking down into the darkness below but with a smile on his face, that seemed to glow brighter than those devilish eyes that once illuminated the murk. Jack smiled back and waved until Julian disappeared completely. Jack suddenly realised that he was much indeed of air or he would drown. He floundered for the moment, trying to get his bearings, limbs flaying in the worlds worst doggy paddle. He stopped closed his eyes and focussed, panic was the enemy, panic was what held him down and caused all the trouble.

Relax. Calm down.

He pushed himself upwards, rapidly kicking his feet before bursting out of the pond, grabbing hold of the pond's wall and dragging himself up. He collapsed over the wall and onto the slabs that surrounded the fountain. He gazed up at the stars as his lungs worked over time to catch his breath and return to regular scheduled programming.

"Goodbye, Julian." He murmured through stuttered breathes and found himself smiling again.

CHAPTER 29

Jack felt good as he traipsed down the corridor towards the staff rooms that once homed cooks, maids, butlers and footmen. Now they stood empty, ridden with cobwebs and lacquered with a thick layer of dust. His wet feet left footprints behind on the carpet, water dripped from him and the robe now hung off him after being soaked through. He pushed his hair back from his face as he continued at his swift pace, his hair appeared darker now and much longer, that when it was swept back it could actually be heard slapping against the nape of his neck. He wore an incandescent smile, a look of pure happiness filled his usually gaunt and forlorn face. He looked like a child who was walking home at the last day of school for the summer. There was definitely a purpose to his stride and he looked confident, he felt it too. He came to a sudden stop outside the staff bathroom. Steam escaped under the door and filled the corridor, cavorting around him teasing him, with its alluring warmth. The silhouette of a female moved across the frosted glass with seductive feline grace, a vision of sensual allure. Jack smiled and puffed out his pigeon chest and smirked with arrogance.

"I'm a man, I'm a man, I'm a man." He said to himself, as he turned the doorknob, astonishingly his hand did not shake.
On the other side of the bathroom door stood the naked captivating hourglass of one Patricia Leon.

"Limp noodle." She smirked, as she teetered half in and half out of her bath. Her brown flesh being kissed by the warming vapour that she wore like a transparent shawl.

"Not anymore!" Jack smiled with a new found confidence oozing out of him that teetered on the verge of arrogance. He strode toward her and seized her in his grasp, kissing her passionately, her eyes widening at first and then closing as their moist lips lapped at each other. Jack could feel her pushing her body against his, her protruding dark nipples brushing on the silk robe only inflamed her want even more. He pushed her away (maybe playing his own little mind game with her) and smiled. She looked down below the loose hanging belt of his robe and whispered something in French as his erect penis appeared through the gaping of the robe.

"I'm a man now!" He said and they embraced again.

It was wild and passionate, he throbbed for her and she yearned for him, as their sweating flesh was consumed by the warm vapour.

Time had lost all meaning to Jack as he came round on the cold tiled floor, staring up at the ceiling, warm vapour evaporating around him. A goofy schoolboy grin sunk into his face as his chest heaved in and out rapidly. His clammy flesh was not agitated by the raw tiles underneath. His penis had risen up and stood proudly erect. It quivered in the aftermath of an enormous climax and discharge seeped out, cascading down his member's veiny shaft and forming a gob of semen that settled in a matting auburn nest. He was alone of course, and any performance that had played out was indeed all in his head yet never once had it feel like masturbation. For the first time, he did not feel ashamed, if anything he felt empowered. He sighed and relaxed and so did his soldier, who had no further need

185

to stand to attention and slowly dwindled to its original state.

"I'm a man now."

CHAPTER 30

Jack had taken the time to compose himself and once again he found himself standing outside a frosted glass door. This time the bathroom on the other side did not contain the pleasures that had awaited him on the ground floor staff bathroom. He stared at the glass panel, and this time his hand trembled over the doorknob. Every time it came close to grabbing it, his hand would retreat. It was not some magnetic force that was causing his hesitation but fear. That word again that appeared before his eyes on the frosted glass in blood, before a gush of crimson moved down and consumed the glass. He gasped and turned away in horror, dry retching in his throat, before turning back slowly and realising that there was nothing at all on the glass. He straightened up and breathed out, his breathing pattern stuttering at first but then levelling out. He knew what had to be done, there was no way that he could leave even one spectre free to roam and haunt his mind. They must all be faced if he were to truly be free of his fears. He reached out quickly, while his nerve was still strong and turned the loose brass knob that rattled in the firmness of his grip. He was in the bathroom, it was plain and clean as if nothing had ever happened. Not a drop of blood anywhere, as if nothing had ever spilt over from the bathtub. Only the sound of the boiler in the airing cupboard could be heard, coughing and spluttering like a sick old man.

"My phone!" Jack cried, spotting his cell phone still where he had left it. He hurried toward it and picked it up. The screen burst into life but then faded to a soft light, the battery almost diminished. He held it up and squinted to see if the signal had connected but still there was nothing.

"Damn it!" He sighed in frustration.

He was about to place the cell phone in the sagging pocket of his Grandfather's robe, but the screen fluttered in a very peculiar fashion. Jack looked at it confused as blood started to drip down the screen from the inside. It filled the screen and Jack held it trembling and gaping but frozen and unable to let go of the phone or even take his eyes off the screen. The screen was consumed by the blood and then it dripped out of the small socket where the charger is usually connected. The blood dribbled onto the linoleum and splashed on his bare feet, he stepped back from it and with a scream he dropped the phone on the floor. Jack backed away from it as yet more blood oozed out of it, creating a large puddle on the floor. The airing cupboard door halted him as he became encircled by a carpet of human plasma. He screamed again as he looked at the floor, that was now smothered with a thick layer of blood. There was a sudden bubbling in the middle of it, which caused the blood to froth, it looked like pinkish spume washing up on a coastline.

"No, no, no!" Jack murmured, the fear obviously still there. The trauma of seeing the aftermath of his Auntie Dilys' suicide had obviously carved several wounds into Jack's mind, they were almost as deep and severe as the ones that she had caused with her razor blade. Slowly a head appeared in the centre of the foam, round and drenched in a thick layer of plasma, it was a sickening sight as

188

though a grown adult were being born in the most callous birth crowning imaginable. Jack wailed, trying to climb up the airing cupboard door behind him as his Auntie's face could now be seen almost skeletal, wearing an expression of nothingness. She rose up out of the blood, smothered from head to foot as if she had been swimming in visceral discharge. Jack stared at her and tried to compose himself but what he saw next terrified him even more, if that was at all possible, She stood naked and motionless. Blood unattractively matting her pubic hair, as crimson droplets fell from the tips of her nipples, the sharp talons of her fingertips and from her nose and chin. Her eyes were bright and burning into him accusingly. There was a turn of her hand to reveal the concealed shard of a razor's edge. It twinkled playfully in what light there was, appearing almost pink from its surroundings. She started to move towards him, long slow strides across the surface of the blood lake that had now formed. It hardly quivered under her wake, it was though it was a part of her and there were no footprints left behind. It was as if she glided over it.

"No, Auntie Dilys, no!" He screamed at her but still she came towards him. The thought entered Jack's head that this is how it all ends and that the outside world would see it as suicide of course. He could see the headlines from newspapers around the globe, about a famous artist committing suicide. They may possibly point the finger that there was drugs involved or depression, not that he died out of his own fear. Fear for all the guilt, low self-esteem and inadequacies that he had faced. Not that the ghost of his dead Auntie had slit his throat with a razor blade. He couldn't let that happen. That was not how he wanted to go out, and it was that that suddenly span him out of his musing. He was suddenly face to face with Auntie Dilys. They stared at each other, their eyes similar, hereditary. Jack glanced down at the razor that seemed to salivate at the prospect of a new victim, blood drooling from its sharp tip. He saw her severed tendons sprouting out of her wrists, twitching like a dying spider's legs.

"No!" He said tenaciously, "This is not what I want! I won't allow this to happen!" He almost growled with authority. Auntie Dilys' expression never changed but her head titled to one side as if asking a question of him, 'What did you say, Jack?' Or perhaps 'I don't understand.' She raised the razor blade in the air but Jack stood strong and fought the urge to grab her arm and keep that blade away from him. He thought that was what it wanted, it wanted him to struggle and fight against it, then it would have him. Yes, it would have him good and scared and ready for the picking, he would be consumed by the fear and then it would strike. Jack did not move, almost coaxing her into making the first move.

"No!" Jack yelled at her and she slithered back a few paces.

"I'm not going to let you blame me. None of this was my fault, it was an accident!"

She looked at him, the whites of her eyes saucer-like in a surround of red treacle.

"Julian's death was an accident!"

She scowled at the mention of her son's name and then blood exploded out of the confines of the bathtub like an erupting volcano. It sprayed all over the ceiling and rained down around them, as though it mirrored her inner rage. She screamed in his face, strings of blood expanding and then snapping as her gape widened

190

abnormally. Jack was terrified, he thought about just closing his eyes and letting it take him, it would all be over then. Maybe he could block her out, shut her away again, lock the door, but she would always be there, she would always come back when his defences were down. He could just let her pierce his flesh with her razor and allow it to glide through skin and muscle, snapping tendons and veins as it finished its heinous act. He didn't, he wouldn't allow any of that to happen.

"Auntie Dilys! Listen to me!" He said, again with authority. She looked at him again tilting her head in an animalistic kind of way of none comprehension.

"It wasn't your fault either."
Her face quivered with the power of these words and her face almost appeared human again. He reached out and placed a hand on her cheek, his palm squelching from the contact of blood. She looked at him, her eyes filling with tears.

"You are not to blame." He smiled and she smiled back as tears seeped out from the confines of red eyelids and cut its way through the red on her cheeks.

"It was an accident and there was nothing no one could have done, never blame yourself, Auntie Dilys, ever."
Suddenly she cried in pain and sadness, the high pitch screech caused Jack to cringe and close his eyes but after a few seconds there was nothing but the sound of the old water boiler coughing behind him. He opened his eyes to see that she had gone and taken with her all the crimson that had flowed from her veins all those years ago.

"Goodbye, Auntie Dilys." Jack smiled.

CHAPTER 31

The terror that had slithered through Jack's veins, freezing him to his very core, this evening was still not enough to crush his spirit. Somehow seeing his Grandfather again, his words had helped put it all into perspective. Was the fear still hidden within somewhere, lingering? Yes, it was. He found it was now manageable. It was almost as if it had lost a lot of its power over him and it was retreating. Even still, the fear could be felt scratching away at his flesh, tweaking the goose-bumped protrusions that had risen all over his body, as he climbed those stairs again which lead to his Mother's room. That thing that dwelled within, that something that he had at first thought may have been keeping his Mother prisoner in some dark cell of despair. The realisation had sunk in that it was no abductor, no evil maniacal being that had her in its clutches, it was only his Mother and what she had become. Floorboards creaked and that Welsh wind seemed to pick up again and swirl uncontrollably around the house. In the darkness all he could hear was the wind and it chilled him to his core, it must have found some crack in the masonry and seeped into the house undetected to rush around the corridors of the house in defiance. Then the ruckus started up again, the bangs and thumps, the sound of glass breaking. His Mother had been woken up and the disturbing sounds were a warning to stay away, like some sort of defence mechanism. It had indeed worked,

Jack had not been back to the room since the first altercation. Even now he felt that sickening feeling in his gut bubbling up like the contents of a witches cauldron. He reached the door, all the while the onslaught on the other side of the door continued. Violently objects slammed into the thick mahogany. Jack took a deep breath that seemed to send a shudder through his entire body.

"Here goes... Everything, I guess!" He said and for some reason he reached out and knocked the door. He remembered being a child and his Mother having these uncontrollable drunken episodes and she would always scream at him to knock, before entering. Jack thought that maybe he had caught her a few times in a precarious position perhaps and could only presume that she didn't want to be seen in such an embarrassing situation. He couldn't remember ever catching her in the midst of her intoxication, he only ever remembered the aftermath. The shouting, no, screaming! The throwing, the putdowns... To Jack the words hurt more than getting caught with a flying perfume bottle or a hairbrush. The ruckus stopped dead when he knocked the door, just silence now, while that wind continued to keep some kind of background noise but from the room there was nothing. He knocked again, it sounded louder this time as though his growing confidence had been transferred into the knocking. Still there was nothing. Jack took this as a sign that the coast was clear and he turned the doorknob and entered. The room was again in disarray, perfume bottles and the contents of her dresser scattered around the room, furniture turned over, framed pictures lay strewn on the floor, glass shattered.

The open window let in a cool breeze, and even with the glass

193

chimney surrounding the lamp, it managed to cause the flame inside to dance from side to side.

"What do you want?" Came the words hissing out from the corner of the room, words spat with venom almost serpent like in sound and delivery. Jack adjusted his gaze to the words and saw a black veiled figure on the other side of the four posted bed, mostly hidden by the untied drapes that fluttered back and forth in the breeze and helped to disguise the ghostly shape. Jack gulped, his Adam's apple descended rapidly down his gullet and ceased irritatingly in his stomach.

"Mother..." He said but before anymore syllables could leave his mouth, the door slammed shut behind him, causing him to almost jump out of his Grandfather's robe.

"Get out!" She wheezed, the letters seeming to linger around the room and slither into his earholes, stabbing at his brain like icicles. Pain shot into his head and yet again he felt that sickening feeling that consumed him at the start of this whole ordeal. To say that this demon, this apparition, this memory was the strongest was an understatement. Obviously this effected him more than anything else... possibly there was one more fear that had plagued him more than this. He would deal with that in due course, because if he could not put this particular haunting to bed then there was no hope of facing the other, he would never be allowed to get near.

"I said, get out of here!" The hovering figure in black wailed and with it came a flurry of items, all slicing through the air and crashing into the wall and door behind him. These objects were being flung at him by no one. His mother was not picking up these items and launching them, they launched themselves as she remained in the corner of the room, wrapped in veil and shadow. Jack ducked and dived, he weaved and dodged, trying not to get hit. He could hear his Grandfather's voice in his head but it was faint, and the words were of no use as they were drowned out by the breaking of items all-around him.

"Mother! I know it's you!" He screamed, trying to be heard over the fracas. The creature clad in black hissed and floated out of the safety of the shadows and swept around the room on a wave of Welsh breeze. Jack did nothing but watch her in anxious awe, she looked like some gigantic raven gliding overhead, black funeral garbs and veil quivering like feathers. She swooped down at him forcing him to cower on the floor, still the bombardment of items broke all around him, she hissed and scolded him with her words. Painful, hurtful words.

"I told you to get out of here, brat! You worthless piece of spit!"

"No, mother, please..." He begged, tears welling up and glazing his eyes.

"You need to leave here! Leave me, leave your Father. We don't want you here, he doesn't want you!"
Jack grabbed at his head, clutching at his ears, as he shook and cowered on the floor, as if his whole body was trying to close in on itself.

"Leave us! Get out! Get out! Get out!" She screeched, the sound was deafening, the words were raw. Items continuously hit him, hairbrushes, perfume bottoms, an atomiser, a jewellery box, a stash box, a vase. It all came raining down on him with force, and he felt her presence swooping over him. Those painful words wheezing

195

out of the gaping black hole that was sunken into her head, where a face would have once sat. Jack tried to focus but it all felt too much for him. She would beat him with her hurtful words like she always had done, and this would continue until the day he died no doubt.

"Died!" She hissed, as if reading his mind but of course she could. She had lived there for long enough now, nestled in its dark corners, keeping the skeletons company.

"Died?" Jack said raising up slightly and seeing her hanging over him like a raincloud, black and masterful.

"Yes!" She wheezed, with emphasis on the last letter as though the word contained a hundred of the letter. He looked up into the cavernous crater that consumed her cranium, almost hypnotised by the swirling of air inside, like some unrelenting tornado. His eyes followed the spinning gusts around and around until his head started to spin.

"Died." She repeated over and over again in that wispy voice and then she moved to reveal the window. It opened up to him and a gust of moist air met his face, blowing back his hair.
The items had stopped hitting him, they now traversed around in the air like trapeze performers at the circus.

"The window?" He asked in an almost hypnotic trance.

"Yes!" Came the catlike reply, "Get out!"
Jack nodded and stood up and slowly walked towards the open window, the words 'Get Out' echoing around his head. The breeze brought with it moisture and it flicked at his face, almost reviving him.

"Get out!" The hissing continued and he stepped closer to the window. He grabbed at the frame and pulled himself up onto the

196

windowsill.

"Get out! Get out! Get out!" She said.

"Wake up!" He suddenly heard as clear as day. It was his Grandfather's voice.

"Get out!"

"Wake up!"

"GET OUT!"

"WAKE UP!" And so it continued in his head over and over again, like two rams hitting heads for possession of a doe in heat. Suddenly Jack opened his eyes and he saw his Grandfather in front of him and he shouted 'Wake up!' once more, as he was drenched with the contents of his glass (which Jack believed to be Scotch) *What a waste of Scotch!* He thought to himself and smiled.

He opened his eyes and screamed, realising that he was hanging halfway out of the window and staring down at that unforgiving gravel beneath. He fell back onto the floor and looked around the room. The items that had been attacking him at regular intervals were now lying dormant on the floor. There was no sign of his Mother but he knew she was still in there somewhere, lurking in the shadowy crevices of the room.

"Mother?"

He stood up slowly and turned on the spot, searching with his eyes. She had retreated back into the corner where she had been originally. Jack saw her shape shifting in the darkness, the lamplight managing to pick out each movement.

"Mother?" He said approaching the dark corner. She hissed back at him like a cornered rattlesnake exhibiting a warning, Jack was not perturbed and carried on with his valiant approach.

"You are worthless!" She squealed, "You are nothing! You have always been nothing and you will never amount to anything." Jack listened, but was no longer affected by her words, he knew now that it was only his own insecurities that he was hearing. Like a lot of creative people, they would all share this fear at some time or another. The best thing to do is ignore it, easier said than done? Maybe, but take a step back and realise why you are doing said creative project. The answer, because you love it! That is really the only reason you will ever need.

"Get out!"

"No!" Jack snapped standing directly in front of the darkest corner of the room. Her vast maw shot out of the darkness and hissed in his face, spittle whipping at his face. The smell of alcohol was choking him but he stood fast and said nothing. She retreated again back into the shadows almost sobbing with frustration and pain.

"It's your fault that your Father was sick and..."

"No! That is enough!" He snapped.

She hissed and whimpered like a wounded animal, seeping into the shadows for protection.

"It's not my fault! None of this is my fault. I am not a failure, Goddamn it I am a success! I'm a bloody good artist!"

He stopped for a moment as if too mull over what he had just said.

"I bloody am, aren't I?" He asked himself smiling.

"You killed..."

"Oh! Do shut up, Mother!"

With each retort from Jack the figure seemed to shrink and the shadow no longer appeared so dark.

"It's wrong of you to blame me for any of this. You have been blaming me for everything since I was a child, that is probably the reason that I couldn't accept that I wasn't to blame for Julian's accident."

She recoiled as if to strike again at this comment, sensing that she could use that past guilt to strike with but he shut her down.

"It was just that, an accident!"

She shrunk back down into the shadow and her shape seemed to change, taking the form of a frail looking figure.

"I do love you, Mother. The way you used to be but those memories are hard for me to find now, because they have been poisoned by whatever this form is that you have taken."

Jack didn't realise that he was crying floods of tears and he sat on the bed dabbing at his eyes with the sleeve of his Grandfather's robe.

"Jack, please don't cry." Came a voice that was soft and gentle, it sounded like his Mother but it was different to what he remembered. It was calm and quiet, there was love in that voice.

"Mother?" Jack said, removing the sleeve from his damp eyes and looked on her with youthful eyes. He felt like he was a child again, swamped in an oversized robe, his bare feet dangle off the side of the bed, unable to touch the floor.

"My little soldier." She said smiling as she appeared out of the shadow. The darkness behind her disbanding, showing his Mother in a loving aura, almost glowing. He smiled at her and remembered her calling him my 'little soldier'. Memories flooded back like a wave, it seemed to wash away all those dark memories and replace them with ones that he had thought lost. She held her arms open, Jack jumped off the bed and scuttled into her arms where they held each other for the longest time.

CHAPTER 32

Jack shuffled into his Father's room, all the time looking behind him expecting to feel his Mother's fermented breath on the nape of his neck. She of course wasn't there, she never would be again, not in that form anyway. He again felt like a child as he closed the door behind him. The closing of the door seemed to cause a vacuum and lock in all those old familiar aromas that used to make up his Father's room. Medicinal smells that stung at his nostrils like wasp stings, but even that was more pleasant than that lingering stench of death and decay that was left to fester in the room, when his Father had passed. The familiar shape of his Father's frail body lay under the duvet, like some rocky landscape. His torso lifting and falling slowly as he dozed away in a world that was surely a thousand times better than the one he was currently in. Jack looked down at his bare feet, childlike and small, almost podgy, not long and skeletal as they appear in his adulthood. The robe dragging across the rough carpet and trailing off behind him like a royal mantle. His Father faced away from him, which is something that he was relieved by. That head turning and unveiling a rotting phantom had visited his dreams far too often. The eyes becoming pulp in the dark sockets of the skull, and the jaw bone dangling from the skull as it jockeyed up and down as if being controlled mechanically. Jack shuddered but moved slowly towards the bed and climbed up on an old chair that sat next to it, where his Mother would sit and weep for hours on end as he slept. As he sat on the chair, legs like two pendulums swinging back and forth. He noticed a piece of paper in his hands, a drawing, it was of course a horse, a black horse. Even with his old eyes looking through the lenses of his youth he could see that there was a talent there in the artwork, even at such a young age. There was no scribbling to be seen on this piece of work, nor were the cumbersome wax crayons of most youngsters drawing attempts used here. Eloquent lines formed with pencil and then caressed in subtle flicks of various colours from pencil crayons. You could see where Jack had pressed harder to create shadow where it needed to be, like his Grandfather had once shown him. He smiled to himself knowing that it was a damn good piece of artwork for a child of his age. He suddenly felt a shudder of fear, even now it still reared its head and why wouldn't it? This was still not over.

"Mother!" He whispered.

He was terrified that she would appear and tear the drawing out of his hands, screw it up and throw it away, along with the words that hurt that he was 'No good' or 'wasting his time'.

He waited but his Mother did not arrive and the feeling passed.

His Father snorted loudly and stirred, Jack held his breath, his tiny fingers clawing tightly into the corners of the paper, where he held it tightly. Too tight.

The moment of truth and his Father turned around to face him, eyelids flickering as he came out of the dreamworld and back to reality. Jack could barely bring himself to look, he couldn't take the sight of his Father looking so weak and ruined, it may just break him.

"Hello, little man." He said, followed by a raw spluttering as he cleared his throat of whatever poisonous tar had clogged it up. His Father's smile was beaming and his eyes shone with life. Jack smiled back, believing that this was the way he wanted to remember his Father. Then his eyes drooped with sadness at the realisation that this was the early stages of the illness and that he would not look like this for long.

"How are you feeling, Daddy?"

"Not too bad." He answered pulling himself up into a seated position in the bed. It was obvious that even this simple task had become a chore, and he fought through it with gritted teeth.

"What have you got there?" He asked looking down at his drawing that was gripped so tightly in his little hands.

"I drew you a picture."

"You did!" He cried with enthusiasm, "Let's have a look at it then."

Jack looked around cautiously, still convinced that his Mother's tapered talon would appear and snatch it away if he tried to show his Father.

"It's okay, Jack." His Father said and Jack turned to face him again, his face had changed, it looked gaunt and almost yellowish, as though his skin had been stained by tobacco.

"She's not here. That part of your Mother is no longer here." They made eye contact and Jack seem to grow all of a sudden and feel like his grown up self. He felt that his Father knew all that had happened and they were now talking man to man.

"Let's have a look at this picture then."

Jack handed the drawing over to his Father, whose hand now

appeared frail, all the tendons rose out of his flesh as he took the drawing, almost spider like. Another look at his face and Jack realised that he needed to talk to his Father as time was being wasted. He was diminishing before his eyes.

"Dad... I..." He tried and then choked, tears swelling now.

"It's a great picture, it really is! This is Black Jack isn't?"
Jack nodded, two matching lines of moisture slicing down his cheeks.

"It's great! What a great likeness! I always used to struggle drawing horses, you know?"
Jack just nodded.

"Could never get their noses right. You should be very proud of that, little man. You'll make a success of yourself if you keep at it. Promise me you will! Promise now!"

"I will, Daddy. I promise."
As Jack wiped away tears he saw his Father had wasted even more, withering before his very eyes.

"Need to watch out for that bugger, Black Jack though."
Jack's eyes widened, it's as if he knew and he flicked a wink in his direction.

"I feel tired all of a sudden, little man." His Father groaned and held out a hand which Jack grasped for and held it tenderly.

"Daddy I need too..."

"Think I need to have another sleep and I'll be okay. We can talk later on." He wheezed attempting to turn over again.

"No, Daddy! Please don't go! Don't leave me again, I can't take it! I..." Jack cried and flung himself off the chair onto his knees and pressed his face against his Father's shrivelling hand.

"Jack."

He looked up at him and his Father was young again, vibrant and healthy looking, a glowing aura shone behind him. Jack smiled, he knew that this was how he wished to remember his Father. This would be the lasting image that would be forever conjured up when he thought about him and it filled him with joy. Just that would have been enough, just not having to picture a rotting corpse when he thought about his Father.

"I'm very sorry that you never got to say goodbye, Jack. That was your Mother's doing, not mine." Jack started to cry again.

"But, please don't blame her, she was trying to protect you. In her own way she did her best, but she couldn't cope with it."

"I love you Dad. I miss you so very much."

"I know Jack, I love you too. But, before I go, I want to tell you how Goddamn proud I am of what you have achieved." Jack broke down, his heart seemed to swell with love, from the recognition and acceptance from the one person that mattered the most.

"You're an amazing artist and just remember why you are doing it..."

"For the love?"

"Yes, for the love. That is exactly why! That is why we do anything. No regrets sunshine, just keep going."

Jack sobbed again into his Father's hand, but when he looked up again he has gone. The room was empty, there are no smells that linger around anymore. Jack sat back on the chair looking around smiling, tears streaming down his face.

"Why was I ever scared? I've lived my life consumed by fear

all of the time, and why? What for? Everything was just in my head."
He shook his head from side to side and laughed a little.

"What is fear, really? A manifestation of our own inadequacies, that is all fear is. All it is! I wish I had faced it years ago I truly do. Now I have, I feel free, like the burden of carrying the weight of the world around has now been lifted. I'm better off for facing those fears. It's something that I must continue to do. I mean what's the worst that could happen?"

CHAPTER 33

Jack had slept the remainder of the night like a log, no nightmares or dark memories to torment his delicate and exhausted mind. He had checked the study before retiring that night, but his Grandfather had gone, 'Of course he had!' Jack had told himself 'He was a figment of my imagination'. Even knowing that, there was still something that made Jack second guess himself. With his travel bag packed and in hand as he stood in the hallway he glanced into the study one last time, he noticed the two used Scotch glasses just sitting next to each other on a small table in-between two weary armchairs.

"Maybe..." Jack trailed off as he stared at those glasses, not really wanting to go there with his line of questioning, because that would put another spin on things. Jack noticed the urn still sitting on the cabinet, he smiled and scooped it up into his arms and stepped forward to open the front door (which no longer haunted him with its perverse knocking). The Grandfather clock in the hall started to tick again, loudly echoing around the hallway, interrupting the silence and breathing new life into the house. He slid out of the house, closing the door quietly behind him. He glanced at his cell phone and the screen was dead. He slid it back into his pocket and walked down the slender steps away from the house out onto the sea of gravel. He let his bag slide from his shoulder and unceremoniously drop to the floor. His hands clasping the urn tightly as he gazed around the grounds one last time. He had a sixth sense that Mr Butterworth would be arriving soon, so he waited. Jack didn't mind standing in such glorious weather, for when the sun was shining in Wales, there was really no nicer place to be. He stared out at the hills and valleys in the distance and smiled as the sun shone down on him, warming him tenderly. In the distance, near to the stables something caught his eye, something large and black moved swiftly across the green landscape. Jack smiled at his Grandfather's name that shined back at him on the urn. Jack quickly left his belongings and started to walk towards the stables up on the hill at the rear of the estate. He climbed over several fences, always looking for whatever that dark silhouette was but he saw no sign of it.

At the stables, which were of course still deserted and in ruin. Jack could swear that he heard the neighing of a horse. He shivered a little as the thought of him creeping into that stable lurked back into his mind but he swept it away, knowing that the sound was coming from the other direction towards the vast fields. Where as a child Jack would climb up onto the fence and watch as his Grandfather would oversee the training of his finest horses. He removed the lid from the urn and shook the contents, the ashes fell out and were immediately taken by the wind, that dispersed it evenly around the stables and fields.

"Goodbye, Grandad." Jack said smiling, "Thank you for everything."

He trudged through the overgrowing grass and came to that same fence that he would straddle as a youngster and in the distance stood a horse. It paced back and forth and flicked its mane from side to side as if Jacks presence agitated it.

"Black Jack." Jack whispered and without a second thought he climbed up and over the fence and found himself in the field, slowly walking towards this agitated stallion that had stopped pacing and was now staring daggers at Jack. He stopped in the middle of the field and asked himself out loud, "Jack, what the hell are you doing?" He had no answer to such a question and he just watched as this jet black horse jittered from side to side, whipping its head up and down and snorting out mucus. Which actually looked mesmerising in the sunlight as each particle was kissed with its glow. It reared up and its clubbing hooves struck the ground and it set off, galloping towards Jack.

"Oh, shit! Here he comes!" Jack said swallowing hard but he didn't move a muscle. He stood his ground and closed his eyes tightly and hoped for the best. He could hear and feel the strike of each hoof tearing up the grass and soil as it came closer and closer.

"Face your fear." He said and opened his eyes just in time to make eye contact with the charging steed, watching as it skidded to a halt and then rose up on its hind legs, with mud covered front hooves flailing out into the air before returning to the ground right in front of Jack with a mighty thud.

"Hello, boy." Jack said reaching out a steady hand to touch its nose, the horse nudged it and then allowed him to stroke him. It seemed to calm him and he settled down. The horse moved slightly and the sun beamed down to show that he was actually a very dark brown colour and not black at all.

"I thought you were an old friend of mine for a second

209

there." Jack said smiling, while he stroked the horse and made a fuss of it.

"How could I ever be afraid of such amazing creatures?" He asked himself as he felt the beating of the stallion's strong heart thumping away in its chest. Jack pulled himself in closer and embraced the horse's large torso, continuing to stroke its warm neck. He heard the heart beating so loud and smiled, it was soothing and comforting. He heard the sound of a car horn serenade and the horse looked jittery again.

"Go on. Get out of here."

The horse bolted away and disappeared into another field. Jack heard the car horn again and turned his attentions towards the house, where he could see an egg shaped figure moving around by the front of the property.

Jack strolled around the corner of the property and onto the gravel at the front of Heron House, where Mr Butterworth and a car was waiting for him. He had his hands clasped to his hips looking around the estate in a bewildered manner, his bulging rotund stomach protruding out of a tweed three piece.

"Ah! There you are, Mr Heron!" He said approaching him with an outstretched hand "I was beginning to be concerned. You haven't been answering my calls and then when I discovered your bag..."

"I haven't been answering anybody's calls." Jack scoffed shaking his hand.

"Oh?" Mr Butterworth grunted.

"I've had no signal and my battery has died."

"Oh, I see! Modern technology, ay?" He laughed.

Jack smiled and laughed.

"How was your stay?"

Jack pondered this question then replied with a chuckle, "Uneventful."

Jack followed Mr Butterworth's lead and strolled over to the car, where he retrieved a file from the passenger seat and opened it up on the warm bonnet of the car.

"I have the paperwork to sign. Found it after all, it had fallen down the back of the filing cabinet! Can you believe that?" He guffawed shaking his head in disbelief.

"Really?" Jack laughed too. He was quite glad now, that Butterworth had misplaced it.

"I'll certainly be having words with Patsy when I'm back in the office."

"No need to on my account. No damage done." Jack smiled.

"So," Mr Butterworth said springing his pen into life with a flick of his podgy thumb, "Would you like to read it and sign?"

"No." Jack replied pleasantly.

"No?" Butterworth enquired in confusion, "You're not going to sell it? Have you had a change of heart?"

"Yes, well, let's just say I have changed my mind."

CHAPTER 34

"It's like you're a changed man, Jack!" Marcy said in jest.

"That's exactly what I am." Jack laughed.

"That trip must have done you some good then."

"Oh, you have no idea!"

The two stood in the gallery looking at the door exhibit, Jack held a pair of bolt cutters in his hands.

"But are you sure you want to do this?" Marcy asked him with a look of concern and bewilderment on her face.

"I'm very sure." He said smiling back at her.

Robin fluttered around in the background anxiously.

"Shall I let them in yet? There's a massive line out there and I think they're growing impatient." Robin stuttered, while he wrung his hands together vigorously.

"They can wait." Jack said casually.

Marcy looked at him, her eyebrows rising up onto her forehead.

"I don't think I have ever heard you say that, ever! And you're so calm? You are usually spinning like a fly without wings, on show day." Jack laughed out loud and gave her a peck on the cheek.

"Oh, how I've missed you."

"Jack!" She gasped and she blushed a subtle red, and batted her eyelids at him coyly.

"There is something I have to do." And with that, Jack took

the bolt cutters and positioned them over one of the links that made up the chain that snaked around the door and frame of the exhibit. The cutters where forced into action and the link was severed. The chain fell to the ground in a heap, like the coils of a dead python.

"There we are! Now it is finished."

"Are you sure?" Marcy asked unsure.

"Yes." He said, turning to her and smiling. He gave her another kiss on the other cheek and draped an arm around her shoulders. She still did not know what to make of this new Jack that had returned from Wales, with a spring in his step.

"Robin!" Jack called. Robin skipped over like an obedient pup, "Could you get rid of this chain for me please."

"Get rid?" Robin asked with some confusion in his voice.

"Yes, just throw it out the back. I no longer need it."

"Okay." Robin said and dragged the mass of chain out through the double doors that led to the staff area. They both looked at the door and then Jack quickly approached it and opened it on its frame, purposely leaving it ajar.

"What do you think the critics will say? The ones that have seen it will know that you've changed it."

"I don't care. They can think what they like."

"But, Jack..." Marcy gasped sounding shocked but was interrupted by Jack.

"When I made this exhibit, I didn't know what it was. I didn't know what it was trying to tell me, but now I do. I know exactly what it is trying to say and I hope that it will now send the message out to the people that come to gaze upon it."

"And what message is that?"

"I'll tell you about it all later on, maybe after dinner tonight."

"Dinner?"

"Yes, I have made a reservation for us at *Esma's* for 9 o'clock."

"Oh, Jack... I!"

Marcy was flabbergasted and blushed again.

"Yes, it's a date. I have waited too damn long and I'm not going to wait any longer. I'm going to face the fear!"

He embraced her and kissed her, the two sunk into each other, fitting perfectly together like two correct jigsaw pieces. Robin arrived and gasped.

"Robin, let them in." Jack smiled and Robin tottered off to open the front doors to the gallery. Marcy stood stunned for a moment and then turned as she heard the clammer of people chattering as they made their way into the new gallery.

"Here they come!" She said.

Jack slid over to the door and launched the door knocker into action.

"With a Rat-a-tat-tat!"

THE END

WHAT IS FEAR?

Fear Trigger is complete, so I turn from the screen and look out of the window. Gazing into a glorious cornflower blue sky, it's beautiful without the imperfection of one single cloud. It is like the skyline from a fairy tale with the sun shining and the birds chirping away. I should be happy by this but then there is that fear that shrouds this proud and happy occasion. The country, the world as we know it has come to a standstill, and we sit in the middle of a pandemic, a virus... a poison has reared its ugly head and remorselessly it is taking lives. That feeling that coils around my chest is fear, plain and simple. Fear of the unknown, fear of uncertainty, fear that we may catch it, fear that we already have it, fear that it will take our loved ones, our friends. Fear that we could die.

I never dreamt that I would be writing any of this, nobody could have foreseen such a tragic turn of events.

Fear Trigger as a concept was born when I started to suffer from some anxiety, my fear of failure and inadequacy and I started thinking how I could combat this entity. Fear is something we all have to deal with, some more than others. I believe that fear is the driving force behind the majority of mental health issues. Guilt,

Anxiety, Paranoia, Low self esteem, personal inadequacies or fear attributed to some kind of phobia, all these issues can lead to depression, but it is the fear that triggers it in the beginning that needs to be looked at. Most suffer from such issues due to events in our past, issues that spend years and years left unattended to grow and manifest into something and when it's ready, it is unleashed, taking you by surprise in most cases. Sometimes we manage to fight back and lock it away, but this is a short term remedy. Like a plaster over a deep wound, the plaster won't stay on forever and that wound shall become exposed again, and the longer we leave it exposed, the more infected it gets.

We need to look at ourselves and ask the question, what are we afraid of? Sometimes that's enough, if you just break it down like that you realise that it's all in your head.Nothing is going to happen to you, nothing. For others it is more difficult to face fears through denial, a lot think they are alone. You are not alone! Everyone has someone to talk to even if you feel you don't have anyone close that will listen to you, there are professionals that you can turn to so don't let that fear stop you from taking that route. Ask yourself what is the worst that can happen? Nothing! Nothing is going to happen. Nothing is going to hurt you. You should never be afraid to show someone that you care and trust what you're afraid of, if you tell them and they don't take you seriously then they're not who you thought they were to begin with. Friends and loved ones will listen to you and give advice if you ask for it, but they'll be there for you. A technique that I have found that really worked for me was to write things down, get those negative feelings and thoughts out of your head before they can manifest into something worse. Keep a log of your feelings and use it as long as you need to. I found I wrote in it every day for a month or so and then I just stopped using it, I no longer needed it. Writing it down you will see it's only words and that they can't hurt you. Don't be afraid of words, good therapy for this is to also burn it after you've wrote it. Don't get me wrong I can lapse from time to time, but it's all about training your brain, taking the reins. So I ask myself one thing, What is the worst that can happen? Nothing, nothing will happen it is only fear and fear is not in control of your life, you are! Face your fear!

To return to my initial opening statement about the virus that is spreading across the globe, it is a scary time and one where it's not our own inner fears that are responsible, it's a fear that we all have and unfortunately it's out of our hands. All we can do is wait, but this will pass, we will beat this and the only way to beat it is to face it.

Daniel J. Barnes

OTHER WORK AVAILABLE

NOVELS

Monster Home
Vatican: Angel of Justice
Vatican: Retribution
Blood Stained Canvas
Maple Falls Massacre
Fear Trigger
Welcome to Crimson
Monster Meals

COMING SOON

Vatican: Unholy Alliance

Visit the website www.djbwriter.co.uk

Follow author Daniel J.Barnes on social media
@DJBWriter on Facebook, Instagram & Twitter.

Proud to be part of the Eighty3 Design family.
For all your website and graphic design needs.

www.eighty3.co.uk

Printed in Great Britain
by Amazon